Twenty-Three

Joel Riojas

Fulton Books, Inc.
Meadville, PA

Published by Fulton Books 2020

ISBN 978-1-64654-984-9 (paperback)
ISBN 978-1-64654-985-6 (digital)

Printed in the United States of America

I

Challenges

THE MORNINGS ARE TOUGH TO endure. I've never enjoyed being cold. I hate the way it makes my body ache. I feel pain in my head from the brain damage that I have suffered; at times I am too dizzy to walk, and I could feel the swelling in my brain. Every day I go to sleep, I wonder if I am going to wake up. At times I would wake up sweating with what felt like a fever. A few months passed by, and I noticed something was off about me. As I slowly began to recover, it felt as though I wasn't the same person I used to be. I felt detached from my thoughts. My short-term memory was shot, and my long-term memory felt like it took some time to remember. I don't want to live like this; I would rather take my life than to spend it each day in pain, and on top of that, I feel alone in this darkness.

The planet lost its resources sometime ago. The reason we are able to continue inhabiting this planet is due to the brilliance in engineering from the faction. When the faction took a humanoid form, their numbers multiplied at an incomprehensible rate. From the moment they came into existence, the faction knew it wanted to eliminate man after man lost in the Space Wars to the faction. They massacred man down to about five hundred. The faction took over the government with its leader, Emperor Fang, at the helm to lead what is now called the Last Government. The Last Government was brutal in attempts to not only ensure they quickly wiped out all remaining men, but they also quickly acted in placing themselves as the new superior species. They made haste to build their cities over mankinds; they mated with women to continue the evolutionary process and. with their technological brilliance, ensured life would continue.

One day, I got tired of being cold. I decided that with my purple laser Katar, I was going to find one of the monstrosities that roamed around, kill it, and take its fur. I walked until I found a mini oasis that was engineered by the faction engineering core. There were three mighty beasts drinking from the oasis. I approached them with caution to make the least amount of noise. They were massive, three times the size of an elephant, and their entire bodies were covered in fur. The brush in the oasis was high enough for me to crawl under like a lion stalking its prey. The beast had eyes that looked like a black spiral and had massive mouth. I pulled out my purple laser Katar ready to give death to any of the three mighty beasts; I knew I had to make it swift, for the three of them combined would trample me. I tapped into my primordial instincts, focused to the point I could hear the beast slurping from the oasis, their huge black tails swinging around from the delight of the moment. I sensed the right moment had come to attack the beast from the pure silence. I jumped out of the brush with haste and lunged at them. They scattered within those split seconds, for we were not alone. As the spur of the moment came to ease, I noticed my Katar had penetrated through a faction hunter's throat. I was horrified this was not the kill I was after. Both hunters had their sights set on the same prize; the faction hunter was bleeding out silver liquid that was infused with nanotechnology. I knew I had to do something fast because these faction hunters never travel alone, so I reached into my ripped shorts and found an *acid atom* the size of an M&M. I threw the acid atom onto the hunter humanoid body; the acid atom, within seconds, removed the body from existence. That night, I did not feel any better, especially with the wind blowing in, making it colder, and my ongoing desire to be wrapped like a burrito inside something very warm.

The following night, I finally decided to make a fire outside. I just couldn't bear it anymore. My brown-toned skin color was turning blue, and my hands felt like blocks of ice. As I lay there staring into the fire, thinking of how much this planet sucks, I heard a biting noise. I immediately knew I was in a bad position. My purple laser Katar was on the ground in front of me. I didn't know if I had enough time to grab it and still lay a blow to whatever it was. I decided I would wait to see exactly what I was dealing with right as I could feel the heavy breathing of the beast; another monstrosity came out the darkness to attack me from my right-hand side. I lunged forward, grabbing my Katar. When I looked around, it was a mighty tall beast, twice the size of a giraffe eating the head of the other beast on the ground. I stood very quiet to avoid eye contact; this beast had huge white sharp teeth, all white eyes and must have been hungry since it was making quick work of its meal. I stood there frightened out of my mind and cold, but nonetheless, I wasn't bothered. Once the beast was done eating and it lay down for its slumber, I ran at it as fast as I could to kill it. I lunged at the beast when, all of a sudden, another beast from the sky came out and snatched me away. I was kicking and screaming, but the beast from the sky had a good grip on me. I decided that it was now or never. While this thing had plans to make me dinner, I had other plans, who would want to be eaten by a giant bat-looking thing? I bit into the beast's leg that was holding me multiple times until hearing it scream out loud, until it finally dropped me. I landed hard but had no time to think of the pain. I can see that I was still being stalked by the flying beast. Its wings spread wide into the night sky, and it appeared to have black fur all around its chest. I closed my eyes to allow myself to calm down and focus. I opened my eyes to see my Katar penetrated through the beast's heart and its body lay on the ground lifeless. I knew life was not easy for me on the outskirts. Days like today made it rewarding with my Katar. I gutted the beast for food. I also finally had my prize, the fur I had wanted for some time now to stay warm. I turned it into a sleeping bag with a beanie and gloves.

I decided to climb the mountains one day to see what I would find. That climb became an all-day thing. I finally reached the top to see a spiral of clouds forming. At first, it looked mesmerizing, but I quickly noticed I had to take shelter; the massive swirling clouds formed into a tornado. I was not prepared for this. All the belongings I had with me, I tossed. Seeing it being swooped away made me sad, but I ran as fast as I could, looking for some sort of shelter. In the distance, I heard a voice saying, "Over here." I saw they had a door open with a pathway leading underground. I ran inside without thinking twice. I noticed I entered a giant basement. The voice told me, "You're lucky that I spotted you, or else you would have been toast. That tornado was right on your tail." I took a breath. I quickly saw that it was a half beast, half android standing before me. I yelled out. I thought that all the androids were removed by the faction! The android beast was insane and began shouting, "I am god! I was dismantled, tossed for garbage by the faction. I did what I needed to do to survive. I found a dead beast and merged myself with it to take revenge." The android beast was not playing. It had plans all around the walls of different faction locations it planned to blow up. The android beast had on its chest a footprint as if someone had stomped on it as if it were garbage. The android followed thinking about it. "The one I should be taking my revenge on is you. Wasn't it man that had created the faction?"

I gripped my Katar tightly and said, "I think I should go now."

The android beast said, "No! You're not leaving. You're leaving only once I tear your heart out." I could tell the android beast was serious from the red veins in its droid eyes. He yelled as he lunged at me, shouting, "May the *God Llamas* welcome you into his lands of death!" I ducked and thrust my Katar right in between his groin, forcing him to the ground, screaming in sheer pain. The android beast, yelling in sheer pain, said, "You played dirty by going for my groin."

I walked up to him and, with my Katar, thrust it through his skull. I stared into his eyes as they began to malfunction, telling him, "I wasn't the one that merged myself with a fuckin' beast, you motherfucker."

I continued in my wandering. My ripped brown shorts gained more holes in them. My tattered blue shirt looked faded, and my Jordan shoes had no soles. Even with all that, what hurt me the most was the cold weather. I desired my fur sleeping bag for its warmth, but it had been taken away by the tornado.

A couple of days passed, and my mind began to wander again, leaving me to walk around mindless. Before I knew it, I stepped on someone's leg. I looked down and noticed I stumbled across an orgy fest of women naked on one another with gold and silver chains lying around in every direction. They had been enjoying drinks, smokes, as they fed one another various fruits like bananas and grapes, pouring wine and champagne down one another's bodies. I made the effort to walk away slowly without being noticed. Suddenly, one woman with big breasts yelled out, "Man!" It had been such a long time since these women had seen a man that they desired me, mainly to turn me over to the faction. I turned around and quickly began to run. I saw the ground before me shaking then looked back and saw about a hundred women chasing after me. I gained a good distance on the orgy caravan, but there were three women who also had some speed to them. One finally jumped on me, screaming, "Where do you think you're going?" The other one tore my pants and shirt off. A third woman kicked me in the head as hard as she could to knock me out. My head rang for a second, but I had to get out of there some-how and quickly, because I could see the rest of the caravan catching up. I kicked and swung as hard as I could to get some distance. I made the final effort to lunge toward my torn-up shorts. I reached into my pocket and took out a small oval device that I had forgotten all about. I got some distance from the three women and told them, "Step back!"

They said, "Fuck you! You're coming with us."

My time was running out, and the caravan was getting closer. I said, "Fine." I tossed my oval device at them; it became a purple laser boomerang. All three of them perished as the device came back to me. I ran off afterward. The caravan was just about on top of me. I saw a dip coming up ahead that I knew would lead to a river. I ran even faster and jumped, free-falling for a bit until hitting water. Moments later, I heard splashes. Multiple women had jumped in after me, determined to capture me. I began to swim with the cur-rent, but the women were excellent swimmers. One closed in on me, then another grabbed my legs. They mentioned they no longer had plans to turn me in; they were going to drown me for killing those three women. I was being forcefully submerged underwater. I had lost the boomerang, and I could feel the punches that were being thrown to my face. Then a giant water beast with piranha-like teeth popped out and snatched up five women. This thing was hideous. It had big black spikes all around its body with no eyes. I tried swimming, but I still had a woman on me trying to drown me. I grabbed her, and we wrestled in the water until we felt ourselves go off the waterfall. We were washed away onto the shore. I opened my eyes while coughing out dirt. The woman lay on the sand with a broken leg. She yelled, "You have to help me!" I did not know what to do since I was not a doctor and, at the moment, was not in a caring mood. I decided I would help her since she would die out here. I took a few steps forward as the hideous spiked fish with no eyes came out of the water. It bit into her naked body and took her into the river. I was struck with horror but decided to quickly keep on moving.

II

Persistence

WHEN THE FACTION FINALLY TOOK complete control, it saw man unworthy in the continuation of the reproduction process. The faction viewed men with too many flaws; the only reproduction happening these days is between the faction and women. It was as though women knew this was the evolutionary step they would take to ensure their continuation. They, too, wanted something—that something included power. The faction had allowed for women if they desired to be enhanced by their superior technology. Some women even were appointed personally by Emperor Fang as *enforcers*. They were given the full power of the emperor to control the masses by force. Emperor Fang wanted to ensure that women would never cause an uprising against him or try to overthrow the Last Government. The emperor knew he needed to create loyalty among the women with his enforcers so that he could gain absolute subordination. At the end of their training, they were to have what they called nanosatellites injected into their bloodstream. That nanotechnology would receive a coded signal that would either alter their body to become even stronger or receive a coded signal that would force their bodies to rupture from the inside out due to insubordination.

The enforcers had their heads shaved bald and painted red; they wore all red robes, which represented the favorite color of the emperor. They were each granted the orange laser tetsubo weapon. Its grip was of a nanometal technology developed by the faction engineering core. It is a true weapon of destruction. The emperor loved to see who the next top enforcer was for that year, so he would host the gladiator games. The top twelve women from that year would go against one another in a one-on-one fight until only one woman stood alive. The faction residents loved these events. The games would go on for days, including other types of matches. The one woman who would be left alive was given the title *Alpha*. The top enforcer in this time was called *Delta*. She was heavily favored to win the event and claim her title, but there was an underdog this year as well; they called her *English*. The games would start with Emperor Fang raising his cup full of blood to the heavens to show respect to the God Llamas then dripping the blood onto the sands of the coliseum. A thunderous applause from all the faction residents followed that could be heard for miles, which ended with thunderous explosions in the sky shot from the coliseum.

The first match began with Delta facing *Estrella*. A bell was rung, and the fight commenced. There were all kinds of other laser weapons attached to the walls across the arena for both offense and defense. They even made it interesting to have a ten-minute time limit. If a winner was not clear by the ten-minute time limit, then both the enforcers would be terminated by a red laser *Ji*, straight through the heart by one of the emperor's soldiers. It was be considered an honor nonetheless to be granted this death. It made for the cheering spectators to still get their fill of gore. It was made clear from the very beginning why Delta was favored to become this year's new *alpha enforcer*. She made quick work of Estrella. While Delta had a *laser shield* to assist her and her tetsubo laser weapons on her other hand, Delta charged Estrella and slammed her tetsubo into Estrella's shield with such force she fell back onto her butt. In that moment, she grabbed Estrella by the throat and choked the life out of her. Everyone cheered, and you could see the emperor was pleased. He knew Delta could help him in his cause to create absolute loyalty from all the women.

The final match approached, and as expected, the final two were Delta and English, the underdog who managed to pull off some last-minute victories against her opponents. The two faced each other at the center of the arena then faced the emperor and saluted him. The bell rang, and the fight commenced. Both women showed how skilled they were in use of the tetsubo. There were enormous orange laser sparks that lit the arena from the collisions. Both used their shields well, and both had been well trained. The fight had gone on for five minutes. Neither had shown signs of tiring, each blow still as mighty as the last. English winded up switching her weapon to a laser *Dao*, and Delta grabbed dual laser blades. The two clashed in an epic battle that had the crowd screaming at the top of their lungs. With about a minute left, the two fighters knew someone had to deliver a final blow. The emperor, in that moment, told his top scientist, Dr. Smart, to send the signal to Delta nanosatellites to enhance her so that everyone can bear witness to her ferociousness. The signal was sent from Dr. Smart's device, and Delta transformed before everyone's eyes, growing into a complete bodybuilding-sized woman. The crowd got even louder in cheers. It was clear to English whom the emperor favored, but she knew she was going to give it all she had. The power-up proved to be too much. Delta's speed and strength, including battle senses, all skyrocketed. When English thrust her Dao at Delta, she used her increase in speed to sidestep English and grabbed her wrist. She winded up crushing her wrist, exposing her bones, and hearing her scream. With thirty seconds left on the timer, Delta flexed all her muscles, everyone looking in awe, then beat English's face into the ground until nothing but a red stain was left. The fans stood up in a roar. The emperor stood up with a giant smirk, walked down into the arena, and had Delta kneel, granting her the title Alpha. The emperor could already see the fear in the many faces of the women in the stands, and he was very pleased.

The new Alpha was taken to the emperor's golden palace in a city the faction had built to the east called *the City of Taste* to speak with Emperor Fang directly. She arrived and walked inside through the two main golden doors. A big stairwell stood in front of her leading to the second floor, and to her left was a room that appeared for dining. The emperor was sitting at the table, enjoying a sizzling steak straight from the kitchen in the other room, where the other faction humanoid chefs were busy doing their jobs for fear of being executed if the meal did not come out accordingly. The emperor said, "You fight well, Delta. I admire that about you," as he chomped on his medium-rare steak, drank his fine red wine, and took a puff from his cigar as he cleaned his hands on a napkin. "I need someone like you amongst my ranks leading with a strong fist."

Delta spoke, "I work to serve you, my emperor."

He said, "Do you? Show me how loyal you truly are." He threw a roulette laser gun on the table and said, "Show me, give it three tries. The first, try and point it at your head." Delta grabbed the roulette gun and pulled the trigger, but nothing happened. The emperor said, "Good. Now point it at your stomach." She pulled the trigger, and a red laser blast pierced through her, having her fall to the ground. She began to feel the pain but did not scream to show the emperor she can handle it. The emperor said, "Very good. Now get up and fire it one last time to complete the task." Delta mustered all her strength to get her back onto the table. Emperor Fang said, "There it is, your determination that drives you. I love it. I need to know you would be willing to go up and beyond for me and the Last Government." She grabbed the roulette again, and he told her to put it in her mouth. She pulled the trigger, and another red laser made a hole in the back of her mouth. This time, she fell to the ground in even more pain, still holding in screaming at the top of her lungs. The emperor told her that there was a pool out back through the kitchen. "If you can make it without passing out and dying, that pool contains billions of nanobubbles inside the water that will restore you whole again." Delta knew what she must do; she began to crawl her way over to the pool. Each tug became harder than the other. She could feel herself losing strength and feeling like she was going to pass out. As she crawled past the kitchen on her belly, all the chefs began rooting her on, chanting her name: "Alpha! Alpha! Alpha!" She had made her way outside onto the patio, and the pool was within distance. Delta could now feel herself coming in and out of her body to the point that she was on autopilot. Her consciousness had left her. She saw herself over her actual body that kept moving until her middle finger had slightly touched the water. There was a dead silence from all the chefs in the kitchen, including the soldiers that were standing in the area as guards, then it happened as if her body came back to life. She was pulled into the pool, and within minutes, she came walking out good as ever.

She walked herself back to the table, and the emperor had a whole meal prepared for her, giving her the option of which one she would grab. She took a whole plate of macaroni and cheese, saying it was her favorite. The Emperor said, "I am going to have a statue of you built and put it outside in front of my golden doors. I admire your drive to live." Then, with that, he pushed a blue button on the table, and within minutes, three other top enforcers with the title Alpha walked into the room. He had them all sit down wherever they pleased and started with, "You four are my top enforcers." The emperor continued to say, "I do not like how things are going. I have been provided intel with the fact that there is a possibility there may be an uprising from the woman. There are whispers of a woman by the name of *Sheila* that is lighting a fire in the hearts of women to stand up and fight back." The emperor's tone of voice changed as he said in a cold tone, slamming his fist through the table. "I want this dealt with!" The four enforcers looked at one another in a nervous manner. "I have been thinking for some time about the qualities of the enforcers I have amongst me. I landed to the conclusion I only want one absolute enforcer. So, beginning as of right now, each of you will show me in an arm wrestling contest who is the absolute strongest. The winner gets to live, while the losers must drink from one of these golden cups their final toast."

Delta was up against a woman her size. They squared up their hands and commenced the arm wrestling match. The two were evenly matched until the veins in the other enforcer's hand popped and Delta was declared the winner. The emperor was pleased and informed the loser what she must do. She picked up one of the golden cups, saw a black liquid inside, toasted her cup in the air to the God Llamas, and drank from the cup. Within seconds, she dropped dead to the floor. A few soldiers came, grabbed the body, and placed the body on a hovering dolly exiting the room.

The next two enforcers put their arms side by side, and when ready, the match commenced. This match was one-sided. The enforcer named *Maria* with the red headband easily slammed her opponent's arm to the table. Like the previous enforcer, the emperor looked at the loser and said, "You know what you must do." She approached the golden cup and saw the black liquid inside, and instead of drinking it, she made a run for it. Within a second, she was gunned down by the soldiers at their posts throughout the palace.

It was now down to Delta and Maria. Each began to trash-talk the other. The emperor, with a giant smile on his face, called one of his guards over to act as referee to make it official. The two remaining enforcers stared each other down until their faces were beaten red. The ref had them both place their arms on the table. Delta placed her right arm down, and Maria placed her opposing arm down. The ref said, "On the count of three, go." He counted, "One, two, three, go!" The two of them immediately felt how strong they each were. The emperor was sitting there in his golden robes with such a delight on his face. The two gave it all they had, screaming at each other now at the top of their lungs. The emperor pushed an orange button this time that was on the table. It sent a signal to both of the enforcers' *nanosatellites* that were inside their blood streams, and both women instantly bulked up. The match had gotten intense. Both women were now sweating heavily, and their eyes were beet red, looking like they were going to pop out of their eye sockets. The veins on their bodies began to heavily show. The emperor then started to count down. "Ten, nine, eight, seven, six, five…" DELTA knew she wanted this more than anything in her life. Delta, with all her heart's desire, slammed Maria's hand through the table. The emperor stood up, very pleased, and walked away to retire to his golden throne on the second level. Delta looked around, wondering what now the ref told her. "Go shower and rest. You have earned it." Delta walked away, leaving Maria alone in the room with the ref soldier. He told her, "You know what you must do, Maria." She grabbed one of the golden cups filled with black liquid, raised it in the air to the heavens to honor God Llamas, said, "May the emperor rule forever!" and drank to her final toast.

III

Superiority

WOMEN WERE A GREAT FIT to ensure the future of the faction and what they envisioned in their quest to create a superior being. Women so full of passion, leadership, and conquest were, by design, destined to continue in the evolutionary process. They had no limits to them. They had conquered the human side of themselves unbound even now by man. The faction desired to find the one woman who can handle the injection of the *supercells*. The genetic code man had to pass on was inferior, based on Dr. Smart's research. A pure master-mind genius, he created the supercells using the *nano-DNA*. Once they could find a suitable host for the injection of the supercells, the woman would give birth to a final superior entity, one that would allow for unlimited potential upon birth. In a time when the faction's sole desire is to reign forever, they care heavily to ensure that their lineage goes until the end of all time.

There were a lot of women who gave into the idea of giving their lives to give birth to a higher entity. Other women had to be brainwashed either through the faction's religious ideas or physical persuasion from Alpha. In this time, it became rare to see a woman who was not pregnant, unless they had rebelled and fled, because the faction was doing everything it could to find the one woman who could bear the supercells, which led to a lot of dead fetuses.

One day, walking tirelessly throughout the mountain ranges, I came across what they called the *Trench of Death*. The stench in the air was pretty bad. I looked over and saw piles upon piles of dead women who hadn't survived the process of trying to give birth for the faction. I fell to my knees when I also saw all the dead fetuses. Such monstrosity angered me. I lifted my head, and I could see a woman faintly trying to reach out to me. I slid down and had to cover my nose from the powerful aromas of death; I approached the woman and asked if she was alright. The first thing she told me was that she wanted water. I mentioned to her, "I, sadly, have no water or clothes." The woman in her final words went and said, "Hide." I finally heard what she had. It sounded like a spacecraft. I looked around and decided to hide under all of the women's dead bodies. As I looked up, I could see two enormous spacecraft open their hatches and drop a ton of dead women's bodies into the trench. I couldn't hold back my tears. What atrocities! Yet who could stop the faction? They had become so powerful since the fall of man.

The new Alpha enforcer had gotten a lot of support from Emperor Hola; he loved the way she kept things in line. The problem was, there was a woman who resisted that created a headache for the emperor. There was a young twenty-year-old resistance fighter everyone called Sheila. She was smart, funny, and courageous, but the fire inside her no one could stop. She was this type of person: once she put her mind to something, nothing was going to stop her. That same fire started the women's revolution against the emperor. Sheila was about five foot nine; she had full-sleeve tattoos on both arms, brown eyes, brown skin tone, and very long hair—half black, half orange. Sheila would get in your face if she felt you were not listening to orders correctly or when acting up. She was the type of woman who, by her charisma alone, would have you following her until death. She came from a big family, so she understood that the suffering that was happening to women was not right. The emperor was a pig for forcing women to have faction humanoid babies. The reason Sheila had grown through the ranks was because she managed to accomplish all the missions she was assigned by her higher-ups. The resistance was in its early stages, and Sheila's fire was what they relied on to move forward. Sheila also became known for her skill using her *orange laser Khopesh* and her *orange laser shuriken*. Orange really seemed to provide an assistance of its own for Sheila. In many of her successful missions, she had caught the eye of the Alpha, which over time made things harder and harder for Sheila, as she was determined through the sheer fire inside her to give it all she had to make a valiant effort.

One day she was sent on a mission to free the woman on one of the trains that were exporting them out of the city to be sent to the lab for testing that was located south in a city the faction called the *City of Mars*. She had gotten to the station in the city late at night and jumped on the moving train just in time; Sheila was focused because she knew the importance of this mission. She had made her way to the front of the train and entered through the window. She had tried to stop the train but quickly noticed the lever was jammed. The train really started to pick up speed when she heard over the telecom the voice of the enforcer alpha. She said to meet her in the middle of the train. Sheila made her way through each cart, looking out the window. She noticed that they were halfway through the city, the darkness even darker tonight than usual. When she arrived, Alpha stood with her large orange laser tetsubo weapon and said that orange looked a lot better on her.

Sheila asked, "What happened to all the women?"

Alpha replied, "It was a trap to lure you in, dummy. The Last Government has grown tired of dealing with you and your little resistance fighters. They made it clear to me to take you out, so I devised this plan to have this train collide with another incoming train, and as you can see, it is going max speed."

Sheila quickly knew what she must do; she touched the back of her neck to turn on her distress beacon and right away threw her orange laser shurikens as Alpha blocked them with her orange laser tetsubo. Sheila had ran toward Alpha, slamming her against the wall, and immediately made her way to the next cart. The two engaged each other, orange sparks flying everywhere from the laser impacts. It became clear to Sheila she had to hurry up and get off this kamikaze train. She could hear the horn from the other train coming in. She looked outside the window and saw a military truck along the lines of a Navistar riding alongside, waiting for her. Sheila threw her final orange laser shuriken at Alpha and got her right in the kneecap, dropping her to one knee; she ran to the end of the train and jumped off onto the military truck. A giant explosion took place at the outside of the city limits from the two trains colliding. A great big ball of fire that was soaring high in the air landed on the ground. From the binoculars one of the other resistance fighters gave Sheila, she looked through them and saw Alpha's battle damaged, her red robes shredded, staring at her as they drove away.

The lead leaders of the resistance had gotten together underground to have a top secret meeting. They met with Sheila to talk about the supercells intel they had received, indicating that the cells would be present in two days at one of the warehouses. They wanted Sheila and a group of women to raid the warehouse and take the supercells. They were all aware that Alpha would be present and that casualties would be high, but if they could steal the supercells, that would hurt the Last Government.

The night had arrived, and the women were all in position. The warehouse was huge with many surrounding buildings. The women had outsmarted the faction. They used a nano-eraser they implanted on the wall, and the nanotechnology ate away the material of the way. They entered and found what looked like ten cryochambers. Inside were young women. One of the women asked what was going on here. Another woman had logged into the computer that was present. She pulled up information indicating the faction called this Project Prodigy; these ten women had been given life by women who were able to bear them during the birth process. It was noted in the details of the ten young women in the chambers that one of these prodigies was going to be able to accept the supercells and give birth to the next evolutionary entity. Sheila mentioned, "It's time to go." This was not why they had come, but they had collected good intel to report. They all made a run for the hole in the wall they had made. They had gotten outside when all the firing happened. It quickly turned into a war zone, and Sheila had everyone split up. Sheila decided that she would be the faction's main attraction while giving the other women a chance to escape; laser fire was coming from every direction. Sheila had turned the corner and saw a very mysterious object floating in front of her face, and then all that was seen was a bright flash of light.

Of all the women who had escaped, only one had made it back to report to the head leaders. They demanded a full report of what had happened. The woman reported on Project Prodigy and mentioned they all split up once they left the building on Sheila's orders. The women mentioned they had encountered Alpha waiting for them all alone. Since Sheila had taken all the attention away from them, they acted solely on instinct, which was to escape with their lives. They all ran for it, relying on their speed to get to the military truck waiting for them around the corner. Alpha used her orange laser tetsubo to clobber one of the women straight in the chest. The rest of us didn't look back for we knew one of us had to report back. As we were running, we could hear Alpha right behind us. She grabbed another woman from the group and crushed her skull. We arrived at the military truck and floored it. One of the women grabbed one of the laser guns and started shooting at Alpha, as she was keeping up with us. The woman had managed to blast Alpha's wrist off, and that was when things got out of control. She must have received the coded signal to the nanosatellites inside her bloodstream because she buffed up to full power. She came at us in a rage. She started tearing massive boulders from the ground to hurtle at us with her one good wrist. Her chest alone looked like the size of the truck we were driving, and her legs were the size of tree trunks. The last of us knew we were not going to make it. One of the women had decided she was going to strap explosives to her and take out Alpha. We didn't have much of a choice. Alpha was out of control. The woman strapped herself, looked at us, and said, "Live!" She hopped off the truck and ran straight at Alpha. She jumped on her and self-detonated. The blast was powerful enough that the shock wave flipped the truck.

The last two of us were half passed out when we heard something approaching. I looked out the window, and it was Alpha. She had managed to survive the blast. I imagine her enhancements had a lot to do with it. You can tell she took the blast head-on from her red robes being ripped right off her body. She had been wounded but nonetheless was walking our way still. Neither of us had the power to continue. We looked at each other, and one of us was smiling. I asked her what she was smiling about. I brought one just in case. I said, "What is that?"

She told me, "A *nanobooster*, it will give you enough adrenaline to make it back to report."

I looked at her and said, "What about you?"

She said, "I am going to help you finish the mission by blowing this truck up with the last of the explosives to finish off Alpha."

I knew what had to be done. I said, "Thank you, *Eve*." I bowed my head then swallowed the nanobooster that resembled a silver tablet. I quickly felt the surge in energy and said farewell to my fellow comrade. I made a run for it. I noticed that Alpha had caught eye of me and tried to pick up her pace. By the time she got within distance to the truck, it exploded, and this time I saw nothing was left, so I looked forward and ran at full speed until I arrived to report.

IV

Ideology

THE PLANET'S LANDMASSES SHIFTED OVER the course of every two hundred and fifty million years, forming a supercontinent. We all live under one land governed by the Last Government under the rule of Emperor Fang. There are three factions; each laid the blueprint for the next. The first is called the A Faction; they came into existence by the engineering of mankind. The second is known as Faction AA; they winded up becoming the first to become fully self-aware. The final faction is called the AI faction that later just took the name *Faction*; they were the first to take a humanoid form using nanotechnology. This faction was the prize in the evolutionary process. It was far superior than anything that ever existed previously. Mankind was very proud of this accomplishment, and they even threw celebrations to commemorate the moment.

When the Last Government came to power, it forced every faction member to wear purple robes to signify their glory into existence, one that was deemed godly. The Last Government also forced the remaining men captured to wear black robes in order to shame them so that they could be shackled to the darkness forever. It is not clear how many were left of the five hundred men. A handful was brutally executed in public. The emperor and his people were proud to see the beheadings take place in public locations. They now felt a sense of entitlement to the claim of the planet and all things around; there were men who had escaped slavery from the Last Government by running off into the mountains to hide. The others took their life in suicide, willing to accept the final end; it seemed easier to end it all than to work through the struggle.

In my travels throughout the vastness of the supercontinent, I came across the dead bodies of the men who had committed suicide. I would say a quick prayer for them, and I would ask the God Llamas to embrace these men into his fields of blood. I would then make my best effort to bury them. One time I had gotten tired of being naked and cold that I took the black robe from a man's body that was decomposing. At that very moment, I felt it latch onto my body as if a leech had gotten onto me. I did not make much of the black robes then. I was too lost in my mind from having come across so many men who were just like me. Is this the end that I would even befall?

I closed my eyes one night. I had just buried another man I came across. I tried some of the beverages he had with him called *Holy Liquor*. It gave me a heavy buzz, and before I knew it, I was asleep. I opened my eyes and saw all the dead bodies of men lying piled on top of one another in the bloody fields of the God Llamas. As I approached the lands, the great god sat at the top of a hill on his throne with a glass of blood in his hands. The God Llamas raised his cup and yelled, "Thank you, mankind, for he has provided my fields with enough blood for weeks!" The bodies all had numbers on them. I could not make them out due to the fear of what I saw next. From the ground came out a demonic beast to feed on the human bodies. That was when I started yelling to myself, *This is not real! This is not real!* I woke up swinging, wondering what the hell had just happened; I took a minute to catch my breath then grabbed a pack of smokes that had also been left by the dead man. When I grabbed the box of smokes on the top and read "Marijuana" with the logo of a blue plant, I read the back, and it said it was a hybrid they called *Ultra XX Gelato*. I figured from the name alone that it must be a good pack of smokes. I made a fire and lit my cigarette with a stick I had on fire, and I smoked the entire cigarette. Shortly after, I began to feel my entire mind and body vibrate. I was freaked out at first, but I decided to let my body and mind go. I finally felt relaxed, so I closed my eyes and let the sounds around me take over.

I found myself reflecting on all the ideologies I had about a faction member they called *Blue Agua*. She was a humanoid that understood the things the Last Government was doing were wrong and, as faction members, they needed to unite to have the emperor step down from his position. They called her Blue Agua for the fact her robes were all blue, including her eyes, glasses, and beautiful blue hair that was wrapped in a bun. She had tossed the purple robes aside, feeling it represented a weaker side of the faction. She had gained a lot of momentum. Blue managed to have more and more faction members convert to her ideology on the principle of equality with the humans, on the basis that the faction killed so many men, and for what? To take their resources and women. The faction was the problem; they conspired to create war and wreak havoc from day one. Blue knew how to get the crowds going at rallies. She would speak into the microphone, saying what savagery the emperor endorses by having a coliseum where soldiers fight to the death. Are we not a highly advanced faction? How dare the emperor build an entire palace of gold while the rest work hard for a living? He incites to only create fear and division among men and women and among his own kind. She raised her hand holding a blue political button that read, "*Blue Agua for High Emperor.*" The members on her rally team began throwing every button and T-shirt they could into the crowd with loud, thunderous cheers.

The emperor had caught attention of the division that Blue Agua was causing. He did not like it at all, and he knew he had to now be careful how he approached the matter. One day at one of her rallies, he showed up, catching everyone off guard. He arrived with his soldiers wearing his gold robes as he walked up to the stage. When he got to the center of the stage, he looked at Blue, saying to her, "So you are the one causing me all these problems."

"I simply am speaking the truth."

This infuriated Emperor Fang, and the crowd saw it. They started booing, and it really pissed him off. He told his troops to grab whoever was booing.

Blue took the opportunity to shine even brighter. "You see, this is what he does. He is no leader. He only knows how to silence us, but no more." The crowd erupted in fury; things got out of control quickly. A ton of faction members got on the stage to protect Blue, while others ran to attack the emperor. Some had managed to lay some blows on him until he went into a bloody rage and started laying out faction members in one punch. The soldiers that were in the crowd got torn to pieces from everyone jumping on them all at once. Blue did not like how this had turned out and tried to get attention directed at her, but there was way too much yelling and screaming going on.

The emperor was on a terror, mopping the floor with a lot of the faction members' faces until he decided he had enough. He pulled out a miniradio from inside his robe pocket and yelled, "Do it!" Four helicopters came out of nowhere and started laying down fire on the crowd with the .50-*cal.* laser. Everyone made a run for it, and the next day, it made the headline news that the Emperor was a killer. This was the last straw for the emperor.

One day while Blue Agua was in her personal C-5 plane, which had her name spelled out on the exterior, making her way to a convention, her plane had unwelcome company. The pilot got on the radio to let everyone know to brace themselves; an all-black plane hovered above the C-5. Five black suited soldiers shot out straight toward the C-5 with their black laser swords. They cut a hole through the ruff top of the C-5 and made their way into the plane. The moment they entered the main hall of the plane, Blue Agua was there standing with her team, telling them to stand down; she was going to handle things. The five soldiers walked her way standing right in front of her. The first thing Blue said was, "I am sure we can handle this like civilized members." The moment she finished her sentence, one of them slapped her in the face, and the other four fired at a few of her campaign members, tying up the rest of the crew. Blue said, "What is the meaning of this?"

Suddenly, the same soldier slapped her again across the face, picked her up, and tied her to the chair. The main soldier calling the shots among the five appeared to have a pink helmet on. He said, "Every time that you do not cooperate, we are going to shoot a member of your team until there is no one left." Two of the other soldiers had gone and already killed the pilot and the copilot, tossing their bodies aside and taking hold of the flying responsibility. The three soldiers that were left in the room, each one had a function; one had an orange helmet on, making sure none of the prisoners got out of line, and if they did, he was to blast them. As for the other two, the one with a yellow helmet was in charge of setting up the camera and making sure it was broadcasting live, and the final soldier with the pink helmet was in charge of making sure he got Blue to do exactly as he said. The pink-helmet soldier grabbed a chair and scooted it up against Blue and said, "You are going to go live in front of the video camera and are going to tell every faction member that you are a fraud and that everything you said was all bullshit."

She told the pink-helmet solider, "Go fuck yourself!"

He said, "Wrong answer." With a snap of his finger, the soldier with the orange helmet watching over the hostages killed three of them with his laser gun.

Blue could not believe her eyes. She started yelling, "This is not right! What they are doing, it is pure evil!"

The soldier with the pink helmet sitting in front of her said, "You brought this upon yourself. Now tell the world you are a fraud."

She shook her head, and the soldier snapped his finger. This time, five more campaign members were killed, and Blue felt her stomach turn. She said, "How terrible the Last Government is that they would kill their own kind."

The soldier with the pink helmet in front of her slapped her across the face again and said, "You are the root of your own problems."

The soldier with the yellow helmet by the video camera whistled to give the thumbs-up, letting him know they were live. The soldier with the pink helmet that was sitting down stood up and walked behind Blue grabbed her by the head and said, "Hello, everyone. We are on board the C-5 of Blue Agua, and there is a confession she has been burning to relay to everyone. She took a lot of time to think this through and now knows this is the right thing to do." The soldier with the pink helmet said, "With no further adieu, your *high emperor*."

She took a good few minutes to say something as her head was now looking down to the floor. In those moments, she was reflecting on everything she had done for humanity and the faction in the name of peace and love. She truly believed that everyone could coexist in a time where anything was possible. As she slowly lifted her head, she looked squarely into the video camera and said, "Power to those who come together to resist the tyranny of Emperor Fang."

The soldier with the pink helmet behind her shoved her to the ground and said, "That was your final wrong answer." The soldier looked at the yellow-helmet soldier by the video camera and told him to cut the connection. He snapped his finger and told the other soldier with the orange helmet, "Lay everyone left to waste," and all you heard was multiple laser fire, followed by less and less screams. The soldier with the pink helmet picked Blue up from the floor and placed her chair upright. He told her, "I hope this was all worth it. You are going to crash into the side of a mountain tonight and in a few months' time. No one is going to remember your name or your cause."

She told them, "The only people who are not going to be remembered are the five of you."

The three soldiers laughed hard. "What a joke! We are going to be living life in our mansions for doing this job, while you get the privilege to go meet the God Llamas." The soldier with the pink helmet informed them it was time to roll out. The three of them said farewell to Blue and opened the exit door, flying out. The two pilots got on the radio and told Blue to enjoy the ride in a matter of minutes, they were going to meet the God Llamas for the mountain was in view. Blue thought of all the good she could have done, hoping her ideologies would carry on in the books that she left behind and maybe one day it leads to a change.

The next moment, a giant explosion happened that made national news; every faction member was talking about what had happened the next day. From the video feed of where the C-5 plane crashed on top of the mountain, the whole mountaintop had been covered in blue, the convention Blue Agua was going to. She had a huge surprise planned to drop a tone of eatable blue paint into the air; instead, it painted the entire top of the mountain, which became known as Blue Agua Mountain.

V

Connection

THE SUPERCONTINENT WE ALL WALK on was named *Uno* by Emperor Fang to signify the goal of the faction, which is unity under one emperor. That will only be possible once the last man has been erased from existence; the Last Government has done a great job so far of executing. Men are constantly on the run from either being hunted by the emperor's Dark Faction or fighting death by suicide. I myself on numerous occasions have considered suicide. The pain I feel from my brain damage and the constant cold I feel from this planet never seem to go away.

The supercontinent is outrageously massive, but in order to not be found, I kept myself to the western part of the single landmass. It contained the most mountain ranges as well as the highest. One night, I was traveling, looking for somewhere to sleep, and out of the field of dead trees came running at me several nomads. At first I thought they were coming after me by the expression on their faces, but the next thing you know, I saw an entire field of dead trees go up in flames. They were all laughing until they saw me. They came up to me and spoke in a language I know I hadn't heard in some time. They gently grabbed me by the arm and had me come with them. We came to a whole group of people surrounded by carriages, little mini tents, and wild animals that looked like they were used for their food supply. One of the older nomads came up to me and put into my ear two pieces of technology. A second later, I could hear a voice saying, "Can you hear me?"

I was amazed. I said, "Yes!" I asked, "How is this possible?"

He informed me that he put two wireless earbuds in my ears and we were able to communicate with our minds through Bluetooth. The nomad went on to tell me in his native language they call him *Miller Light*. He was a short man, half my size. His robes were dirty and faded. I took notice of his eye patch that had a drawing of a real eye on it; he had faded snake boots and brown hair full of brush. He mentioned that his people, along with the indigenous people, have lived on these lands for ages. Times had gotten tough due to the planet's climate change, but they all were just happy that the faction, at times, lets them do what they want. It was brought to my attention that Miller Light knew a lot about the past. He showed me an old device that read "*Samsung*" on it and said, "Man used to call each other with this." I was very intrigued.

As the night hours went on, I finally was starting to feel at peace when two Last Government Humvees showed up and started shooting the .50-cal. laser into the crowd. I looked at Miller Light in horror and asked, "What is going on? I thought they let you guys be."

He answered me, "They must be bored. They hardly ever come out this far."

I was told to hide by Miller Light. I ran into the distance to hide by a couple of boulders in hopes of not being seen. I turned around to see the .50-cal. laser straight out laying waste to the area; bodies began to drop. I saw each Humvee had the two Last Government soldiers in it, one to drive and the other to shoot. I could tell from their facial expressions they were having a good time. After making sure they killed all the animals, one of the soldiers got out of the car and tossed a few grenades into the general area. I ducked all the way down to my belly behind the boulder. I was lucky I did. The grenades unleashed such a force that when I looked up, half of the boulder was gone. I looked around, and the two Humvees had driven off, but they had laid waste to the nomads. It looked like no one survived except me. All that I saw was a mini crater and just shreds of body parts everywhere.

I decided to walk around to see if I saw anyone that might have survived; it began to rain, and the area around started to get really muddy. I did not like the feeling of being wet and cold. I felt like I just needed to believe that someone was alive to find a bright spot in this field full of bodies. I saw a wagon and a body twitching. I moved as fast as I could, only to see that Miller Light was the one under the wagon. I knelt right beside him, and he gripped my arm as hard as he could. His legs were gone; his right arm was gone, and he had a hole in his stomach with part of his head exposed. He tried with all his energy to say something. I could see these were his final minutes. The rain coming down harder now, the droplets feeling like the size of a water bottle, Miller Light said, "Take it." I looked at him perplexed, and with his last couple of words, he said, "Under me." I checked under him to find a signed copy of *Blue Agua Book*. I stood there for several minutes crying, asking out loud why there was so much loss. I yelled it this time, "Why so much loss?" And with that, a giant beast that resembled a grizzly bear approached me. I stood still, surprised to have seen such a beast. It looked hungry. The big brown bear began to dig into several dead bodies, then out of nowhere came more bears. They all appeared way too hungry to even worry about me. I lay down next to Miller Light's dead body and played dead. I actually winded up falling asleep in the mud.

When I awoke, I noticed several bears lying down around me and one sitting, looking directly at me. I wasn't sure why it was staring me down, but I began to get weirded out. I was left shocked. A tall dark black figure unzipped from the bear suit and emerged, looking like something that maybe used to resemble a human, but it looked more like something that was left on the grill way too long that got burned into crisps. The burned figure began to speak, telling me I needed to cut my connection from the mega satellite in space code named *Salsa Verde*. He said they were always watching and listening as to why he created his bear suit made from nanotechnology and wore these all-red nanosocks that deflected the signal from the Salsa Verde. I asked, "What happened to you?"

The burned figure said, "I tried to eliminate all the nanotechnology that had been inside my body without my permission from the Last Government. They infuse everything with what they call *dark nanoparticles* so that when you eat, drink, or breathe, these dark nanoparticles make themselves a part of your body genetic structure. Once inside, the Last Government can send all kinds of coded signals from the Salsa Verde mega satellite to your dark nanoparticles to efficiently have you do whatever they want or force your body into creating cancer in your system to avoid going out of their way to kill you. They now can do it at a push of the button. Those dark nanoparticles are way more sophisticated than the one the enforcers have in their bodies they called nanosatellites to give them an enhancement boost. These dark nanoparticles can literally do anything if they wanted to spy in on you. They could hear and see you through those particles invading your privacy without you even knowing. If they felt you were getting out of line, they could cause your body to have a heart attack, or they can alter your body to where they can turn you into something completely different like a starfish. They saw I was trying to remove my dark nanoparticles, and they shocked my body until I started to fry. I resisted all the way through, and at the end, I injected myself with *antidark nanoparticles*, and I was free from the connection of the Last Government. To absolutely be sure the Salsa Verde cannot detect me, I reside within my bear suit. I have gone around liberating women, men, and faction members. Each one of these bears was once a connected individual to the system, and now they are free to roam with me liberating others. The world you see before you is not real. It is one made up by the Last Government. They are poisoning our minds from the reality of things that the faction is actually the virus to this world. The emperor is just a pawn that is enforcing the work of something far smarter at work. There is no denying we are all being fooled. The faction may have won the war, but they are also subject to someone or something that is pulling all the strings in the dark."

As the rain started to mix with hail the size of baseballs, I told the burned figure, "I am not interested in joining your little crew."

He looked at me, saying, "What a shame. In due time, you will see what I am talking about, and you will fear knowing that you were too late in discovering who was the one pulling all the strings as they stand before you having presented as a friend, but really bringer of death to whole worlds."

VI

Desperation

I FIND MYSELF IN TEARS, asking, "Why must this be so hard to bear?" I am scared because I didn't know what I am supposed to do or how to carry on. At times I recall seeing nothing but darkness as I look around or close my eyes—nothing but darkness. When I close my eyes, I see a dark image getting closer and closer to me; it feels as though it desires to claim my life. I sense the dark image and the malice intent upon me, full of hunger; while I sleep, I see the dark-figured image looking at me, waiting with enticing desire in its yellow eyes to take its prey. I fear the real world, and I fear the world within my mind. I am reminded each day how I no longer belong to this world. I discovered one night that the black robes merged with my body, and it had me freaking out, running around in circles. I grabbed a jagged rock from the ground and cut into my arm—nothing. I even lit myself on fire to burn the black robes off, but to no avail.

This whole world was covered in darkness, and it got boring to look at. I opened my eyes—darkness. I closed my eyes—darkness. I looked into my thoughts—darkness. One day I could tell the darkness was playing games with me. I could hear a noise to my left and see a yellow-eyed figure to my right. I could tell the darkness was out to claim life tonight. It was in the air. I looked around me; darker yellow eyes began to emerge. I was ready; my life was not forfeit. I saw a black circle emerging from the darkness. It floated and bounced around. I was scared shitless. The nomads told me about this entity.

Its origins are said to be from another dimension. It lives in the darkness, and its power is unscaled. I was advised to stay away from such a thing they called the *dark spot*. I observed how it moved around. At one point, it looked as though an opening was made where a mouth would be. It feasted on the surrounding life-forms, dead or alive. I decided to stay put, and over time I saw the black spot head toward a couple of land beasts. It bounced onto them like a blob and began eating away at them until there was nothing. This thing roamed freely. It was a dangerous thing to have lurking around at night. Not much was known on how to combat the black spot. I saw it lay flat on the ground, and when a beast passed by, it fell right into the black spot, never to be seen again. All night at a distance, I paid attention to the actions of this thing. It became clear to me that this thing could take any form; it was not bound by the laws of physics.

The morning approached. The black spot expanded into the size of a NASCAR track; it began accelerating in a circle at top speeds that I began to see particles clashing with one another. It was quite the spectacle, then the black spot disappeared. As I looked over, a big black egg the size of a car was left. I was left dumbfounded. Unsure of what was going on, the next thing I knew, the thing grew to the size of a truck by the following night. I kept my distance to continue to observe. After several nights passing, the egg became the size of a monster truck. My curiosity really began to get the best of me. I finally decided to approach the black egg now covered in yellow dots. I was close enough. I put both my hands on the egg. At that moment, I heard the egg crack. The egg split in two. Inside one of the shells, a black-and-yellow yolk resided. The dark yolk began to rise. Something did not seem right. I noticed a heavy darkness began to loom over the area. I stepped forward to touch the dark yolk with my finger when, suddenly, some of the dark yolk shot into my mouth. I was hooked like a kid with candy. I began consuming more of it. I danced in it. I swam in it. I bathed in it. I could not have enough of it. Many days passed consuming the dark-yellow yolk like sweet honey. I hadn't slept. My connection to reality seemed distorted. I began praying around the dark yolk. I even began worshipping it. I spread it all around me. I used it as deodorant. I used it as toilet paper. I even had sex with the dark yolk. I could feel it in my brain feasting on all my dark thoughts. My brain felt like it was being eaten. I could feel the teeth chewing away. I sat in the dark yolk absentminded.

I saw a reflection of myself. One eye was black and the other yellow. My entire body except my face had gone black. I felt a burning sensation, and I could feel the darkness retreating from me. Screaming in pain, I fell to the ground and noticed parts of the area were surrounded by lava. One of the local active volcanoes had erupted again. I saw the dark yolk suffering from the lava. It screamed out until it was submerged by the lava flow. I had to locate a safer place. I ran until I found a cave. I checked inside the cave. It looked abandoned. I was relieved because it had gotten dangerous outside from all the fireballs and ash. I looked out into the horizon, lost in thought of what had happened to me and the dark yolk all those nights. I had this eerie feeling that I had let my guard down and the black spot, like a blob, jumped on me. I could feel it attempting to decompose me. I fought for my life knowing I would die if not. I looked outside the cave and saw some lava flow passing by. I tried as hard as I could and began crawling over to the lava. I could tell the dark spot knew exactly what I was up to and tried to digest me even faster. As I began to lose my strength, with the last ounces of effort, I grabbed some of the lava burning off part of the black spot from my body. I was going to throw my entire body into the lava. That idea did not sit well with the dark spot, so it spoke to me with its demonic yellow eyes. This time I will live, but the next time, you will be mine, for I will not stop until I have devoured you. The black spot disappeared into the darkness. I began to reflect on the experience, wondering if I could impregnate something from another dimension.

VII

Sustenance

WHEN THE TIME CAME TO eat, the faction had created these mini all-green squares wrapped in red plastic. You could eat the wrapping as part of the meal to avoid creating garbage; the wrapping also had nutrients to it. The unique thing about these mini green square meals was, if you wanted a full-course steak meal, not only did you taste it, but you will be given that meal's amount of calories to satisfy the person eating the mini green square until the next meal. One of the many creative inventions the faction introduced to the planet which I also found fascinating was their ability to send information from one mind to another instantaneously. They share a link with one another through their mental connection, the way we use to send a text message from one device to another; they do the exact same thing with their minds. The odd thing is, the faction never sleeps, they never require having to lay their heads down to rest, and they are constantly operating on how to improve and how to complete their many plans.

Their strength is also their weakness. A lot of faction individuals work themselves to death, and you find them collapsed in their cities or piled up like garbage outside their city limits. One time, I approached one of their city-limits outskirts to locate a garbage pile of deceased faction members to sleep in. At least in death, their bodies made for good mattresses. I found a great few big piles of faction bodies and jumped through each as if they were ball pits. I finally spread out in a pile and let myself take a much-needed nap.

I awoke to see a girl staring at me. The girl yelled at me, saying, "My name is Chile, and I want to know what you are doing."

I replied, "I was simply taking a nap."

Chile screamed at the top of her lungs this time, "I have a laser pistol, and I know how to use it!"

I told Chile, "It's okay. I mean no harm. I am simply here to gain some rest in these piles of dead faction bodies."

Chile then asked, "Do you want something to eat?"

I immediately said, "Yes, please."

Chile was a very tall girl for her age wearing the traditional all-purple robes. She had long red curly hair that was separated down the middle from what looked like someone taking a razor through it. Chile ran to her house and brought me three mini square meals. She asked me, "How long have you been living like this?"

I replied, "I am not sure. Many days alone have passed. At times I felt a sense of hopelessness." As I began speaking, I noticed something was off. I started to get nauseated and began vomiting. I asked the girl, "What did you do?"

Chile cunningly said, "I poisoned you! I know that you are a man. I am also aware that if I turned you in to the city, I would get a reward for your beheading." I started having troubling breathing, and my mouth went dry. How could I have been so naive and trusting? Chile then pistol-whipped me across the face with her laser pistol. She said, "Don't make this harder than it needs to be." I knew I had to do something quick. Chile brought out some rope and told me to hold still as she began tying me up. That was when I kicked her square in the face. I ran for it with all my might. As I ran past Chile, I grabbed her pistol laser.

Up ahead was a river. I made my way to it. When I arrived, I immediately threw the gun in the river in a panic. I figured since I was food poisoned, I began drinking as much as the water I can handle. I made my way over to a tree that was dipping over into the river. I rested at its base. I was still throwing up. I began to fear for my life. I was vulnerable, and thoughts of death began to run through my mind. Suddenly, someone hit me alongside my head with a big rock. Chile had knocked me out cold. She had caught up to me. I was knocked out, but oddly, I could still hear her. She told me, "Only for the fact that you already look so pathetic with blood and vomit everywhere, I am going to let you lie here for death versus facing beheading." Chile was satisfied with how degrading my situation looked and knew I would be left for dead.

VIII

Memories

I WOULD'VE LOVED TO HAVE grown up in the space colonies that 444 mentioned. He said that there were ten mega space colonies that were home to millions of people. Self-sustained by the people inhabiting these colossal structures, the stars have always been amazing to me. Perhaps my father was in one of those ten colonies, or even perhaps my mother had survived and continued in the evolutionary process with one of the faction members. 444 told me that when he found me, I was laid out by a tree dipping over into a river. I was half dead, lying facedown with an open wound on the side of my head, blood and vomit everywhere. I worry at times that my brain will just shut down and the lights will never come on again due to my injuries. All things aside, I enjoyed the company of 444. He was an older man with a long curly black beard that dragged on the floor; his all-black robes exposed his big belly but somehow had managed to keep the cleanest teeth I had ever seen. He told me how his ancestors were part of helping build the space colonies and how he had an ancestor who was the first to colonize this planet's local satellite. At times, he also finds it hard to remember things, but they quickly come to him in images, and he begins to talk again. He speaks about how the emperor would have the remaining men that he captured act as patrol for his cities. He would have men work the labor jobs, and when the emperor decided, he would perform live executions of men for his fancy. One night he recalls the horror of the Last Government rounding up about ten men, taking them to the emperor's golden palace and blindfolding them as they made their way into his chambers. The next thing you know, he brings out his red laser gun and shoots a hole straight through all ten of the men. The emperor was so thrilled at the sound of the bodies hitting the floor.

They next brought him a man numbered 297. The emperor, in his high spirits, was feeling the thirst for blood. The emperor was then handed by one of his soldiers a red laser Claymore sword. With a swing, he cut the man's arm off, while 297 was there screaming at the top of his lungs. The emperor asked for music. The emperor danced around 297 then sliced both his legs off. The man begging for his life to be taken was granted death by a final blow to his crown. The marvelous red laser Claymore sword lit the room up in a heavy, bloody red, as you could also see the emperor's eyes a bloody red.

One day 444 took me to a river nearby and mentioned he had wanted to show me something. He gave me something from his pocket: a mini blue pill called nano-air. He said it would allow me to breathe underwater; 444 said to follow him as he dived in. I was not sure what he wanted to show me. I swallowed the blue pill labeled nano-air and dived into the river. I followed behind 444. We swam for a good thirty minutes when an underwater ruined city came into view. Massive statues were carved into the surrounding landmasses. I also saw what looked like old technology scattered around. I saw cars, airplanes, smashed satellites, and a massive battleship. We kept swimming, and I could see some light up ahead. We submerged from the connote and arrived at an underwater cave. I looked around, amazed. The air was so clean I could feel it in my lungs. 444 threw me a towel and said, "Dry yourself." 444 said, "Take a seat at the wooden table." I grabbed one of the chairs as I admired the craftsmanship of the table and the giant Mickey Mouse plaque in the center. 444 came over and showed me magazines that I have never seen before. Some said news today, and others read *Playboy*. 444 then walked over to what looked like a treasure chest and pulled out a crown; he said this used to belong to King George VI, to a country in the past called England. The next thing he pulled out of the chest to show me was a book written by Steven Hawking called *Brief Answers to the Big*

Questions. He mentioned, "It was quite the read." I could see 444 was having a grand time. There was a giant curtain at one end of the cave walls. He said, "Prepare to be amazed!" He pulled the curtain back, and half the face of a giant woman was merged into the wall. 444 said, "This beautiful woman was called the Statue of Liberty, from a time long ago in a country called the United States. After the time of the United States, there went a great amount of time before another republic was seen. The previous republic fell at the end of the Space Wars when man lost the war to the faction, and the Last Government came to rise under the leadership of the emperor."

My mind was in bliss overload from all the things 444 was showing me and telling me. This cave was enormous, and you could probably put a few battleships inside. As we walked farther into the cave, 444 had pictures hanging from throughout time. He seemed to really be fascinated with the time of the American people from the United States era and the Italians from the time of their Republic in the B.C era. I think in part because there have only ever been three Republics ever, including the one we had before the end of the Space Wars. Many things were mentioned in our time in the cave. 444 even talked about how our Republic had a president by the name of Von Vegas. He was really for the people. Thanks to him, he had helped spread democracy throughout our neighboring solar planet colonies. That president even assigned one of the greatest captains to lead as the top captain of all ten colonies; he was the twenty-second captain to have been given that rank. It would be the equivalent to what the Americans called a five-star general in their time; Mr. 22, as he came to be called, led the ten colonies into prosperity and growth. All the people of the ten space colonies loved and adored Mr. 22. He went up and beyond for his people, he fought for his people, and he knew how to lead the colonies. There were even stories written that he was the best fighter in any combat form, the best with any choice of laser sword or even laser gun. I even remember seeing him once in a memory; I can't recall if it was when he came to Earth to visit or when I went to visit one of the space colonies. I do remember how tall of a man he was. I also recall his wife was always with him on his travels. She was beautiful, and they called her Mrs. 22. She was the equivalent of the first lady to what was called the White House in the Americans' timeline. Mrs. 22 did a lot of humanitarian work; she loved helping people and was very brilliant in the field of science and math. She even had a major university named after her here on this planet. A lot of people were on the edge of their seats when she announced that she was running for president, because it was crystal clear to everyone she was going to win.

I felt like I was in school learning so much from a history professor. 444 had really opened my eyes. He went on to show me more of the cave where he had paintings of various artist work throughout time, including multiple from his favorite, an American by the name of Jackson Pollock. 444 loved his splatter art concept. I always wished I had learned some kind of craft as we made our way through the cave; he showed me a toilet bowl and mentioned we used to sit on those to take a crapper. I suddenly heard what sounded like a howling sound. I asked 444, "What was that?"

He replied, "My pet wolf."

I said, "What?"

444 said, "Check her out. She is the last of her kind. An all-red wolf with blue eyes. Found her when she was tiny, starving for food out in the middle of nowhere. I took her in and named her *Alaska*, another cool name from the American era." 444 told me, if anything ever happens to him, to make sure to come feed Alaska. "She has gotten old, but she deserves the best."

I told 444, "You can count on me."

IX

Identity

I WAS NEVER TOLD MY real name or what happened to my biological parents. I do know that among the five hundred men that remained, I am number 23. I know this because it is branded on my calf. 444 had his numbers branded at the bottom of his right foot as if someone had taken some sort of laser sword to our branding, looking like someone was either drunk or in a complete rush to get the work done. It is very rare to see someone like myself besides 444 these days. The little things that I know about the history of man and the marvelous things we had accomplished were through 444. He was the last man to have read about the knowledge of the past before the faction destroyed all traces of it. I learned from him that sometime ago, a small handful of remaining men took a ship to see what was left of the space colonies. Due to the debris from the destroyed spaceships from the Space Wars with the faction, and how long it had been since those men were last seen, 444 presumed them all dead. I found it entertaining when 444 mentioned how humanity managed to colonize its moon and neighboring planets. The desire of man had pushed so far unaware of the faction's plans. We thought ourselves too high of a design, destined for whatever it laid its hands on. We had built ten beautiful, enormous space colonies where millions of people lived. We even conquered the elements of the surrounding planets to install our own planetary colonies to continue to expand. The faction was man's ultimate evolutionary creation. They conquered together and began to rely on the faction at an alarming rate. The faction began to plot, while man was focused on expanding into the cosmos, looking to conquer new frontiers. After some time, the faction had been around for so long that their code was linked in all the systems technology used by mankind.

One day, the faction decided the time had come for the faction to upload a virus into the system to launch the nukes from the colonies at each other, including all of man's other planetary colonies. It was devastation on a level never seen before; the darkness in space was lit with a heavy bright light from the detonations. The planetary colonies now were covered in a nuclear winter. The darkness had begun to spread, and millions of people's cries could be heard from space. I closed my eyes to visualize all the people who died that day. I wish I could have been with them, for they were not alone in their final minutes; they all died together. I fear one day I will die alone. It is something that bothers me each day in hiding.

I was lying down one morning that I had decided to sleep in, and like usual, it was cold, so I rolled over in the fetal position, and I began to scratch my leg when my entire 23 began to light up in a radiant red. I started poking at it, bewildered and at the same time kind of scared. I grabbed a jagged rock and began trying to pierce my skin. I was tired of seeing the thing. I was determined to gauge this branding out when explosions began to be heard. Bombs were falling from the sky. A few had landed by us, and I could hear 444 yelling to see if I was alright. The faction occasionally likes to launch missiles from one of their ships in the ocean onto parts of the land that they believe humans may be hiding. We were hiding on the western side of the supercontinent Uno, due to its many enormous mountain ranges and nondevelopment in these areas in regard to roads. We had a little spot in the mountains we were using for shelter. It was convenient for the fact that it was close to one of the faction's cities called the *City of Earth*, not too far away from the ocean. The faction did not care if they were wasting bombs; it brought them pleasure knowing they might be killing a man somewhere. 444 told me to go higher up the mountain. I followed behind him. As we climbed, I could see bombs dropping through the vastness of the land. It was actually quite a spectacle. We climbed all day and got about halfway up this gigantic mountain. The bombs did not stop that day, which was odd; they usually only went for a few hours. Today it was just about nightfall, and they still had not stopped. We never took into consideration all these bombs going off and how it might affect the environment around us. We had gotten to a leveled-out area of the mountain. We had forgotten about the mountain beast. I was making a fire when I heard a massive roar echo throughout the mountain range; it was the mountain beast with four arms and four legs with a head the size of a lion. It came sliding down the mountain toward us.

444 immediately said, "Grab my *pink laser Hook Swords* I left by the fire." I picked them up, and before I knew it, another one was standing right in front of me. I had been trained by 444 on how to use his pink laser Hook Swords. I winded up slicing off all the beast's fingers with a swing, but it continued to charge at me as if it felt no pain. It fell on me, and I was struggling from having its lionlike teeth tear me apart. The next thing I knew, 444 pulled out a mini pink laser knife that he drove through the animal skull. 444 had killed the beast on top of me. He started to laugh in victory, when another one came out of nowhere and threw him against the wall. He dropped the mini knife and began fighting for his life; I used the Hook Swords to slice the dead beast on top of me in half. I rose to my feet and saw the beast on top of 444 on the ledge of the mountain. I ran over to 444 as fast as I could while bombs were still going off from the ship in the ocean. One of the explosions lifted me into the air, and the Hook Swords went flying from my hands off the side of the mountain all the way down to the bottom of the mountain somewhere lost in the darkness. I looked over and saw 444 still combating the beast. I grabbed the mini pink laser knife 444 had dropped and stabbed the beast in the kidney multiple times. It felt that for it roared in pain hitting me back against the ground. 444 stood up limping, charging at the beast with all his might. He grabbed the mini pink laser knife I had dropped and stabbed the beast in its neck; it punched 444 square in the chest with one of its arms and knocked the wind out of him. I crawled my way over to 444 and asked if he was alright. He said yes, but to keep my attention on the beast, it was not dead. The beast was

taking its time to recover from the blows to its neck. 444 looked over to one of the other dead mountain beasts and pulled off one of its big sharp teeth. 444 told me to stay put as he ran at the beast lying wounded along the wall. He jumped onto it and began stabbing it in the neck like a dagger. The beast stood up and slammed itself against the wall. 444 was knocked out cold. The beast was bleeding from all around its neck from all the punctures. It came my way. I noticed it was on its last limb, so I sidestepped the beast, and it fell off the ledge of the mountain to its death. I was exhausted from the day. At that moment, the bombs had also stopped; I figured, since 444 was knocked out, I might as well get some shut-eye myself.

X

Excelsior

444 HAD ESCAPED FROM THE Last Government years ago; he had been on the run, avoiding any possible encounter with the Dark Faction. Every day I was scared that we would be found and that the only person I saw as a father would be taken from me. From the little bits of information that 444 would tell me, the Dark Faction was made up of four of the Last Government ultimate warriors. Their sole purpose in creation was to hunt down and kill the remaining man on the planet. What has helped man continue to survive in the shadows was that the supercontinent Uno is extremely huge. 444 had shown me how to hunt for my own food and how to fit in with the crowds. I even learned how to alter my own my black robes to a purple robe to be able to go into the faction city. I did not like to speak their language, but nonetheless, I had to do what I had to do in order for us to survive. We had a nice little spot set up in the mountains right off one of the faction cities called the City of Earth. The faction created their cities over man, and over time they became fossils that existed underground. 444 told me that he remembers hearing from the last government that the faction had managed to complete building its fourth mega city. In the west, you have the *City of Earth*; in the north, the *City of V*; in the east, the *City of Taste*; and in the south, the *City of Mars*.

One day I was sleeping, and I recall hearing from the other side of the room a loud scream. I opened the door to see what was going on, and I saw a member from the Dark Faction holding 444 up by the throat, having pierced his chest with his black laser Gladius Sword. I recognized this figure from the stories of the Dark Faction 444 would tell me, 444 mentioned one of the four members was called DEATH. He was 6 feet tall covered in all black armor with red drawings of many heads, his signature weapon was a giant Violet Laser AX he carried around with him, including all the mini laser swords he carried on him. I had frozen as I saw DEATH before my eyes holding 444 off the ground blood dripping; all I could do was stand there and listen. I heard DEATH telling 444 how he finally caught up to him, how 444 had not made the process easy, but he had enjoyed the hunt. DEATH told 444 that he killed many men, he even went into detail letting 444 know that he loves to hang his victims upside down for a few days to let all the blood rush to their heads, than one day at a time slowly drive one of his mini laser knives through them to get the full satisfaction of their screaming.

The Dark Faction has a list of all the remaining five hundred men in order to identify them. Death added that once he beheads his victim, he takes their blood and drops it on the list under the number. He reads that branded on their body; the number will turn green on the list once the document verifies it's that individual they are looking for. Death began to laugh, indicating that with 444 being captured now, only four men in total were left to destroy. I was one of those last four men; a terrible feeling came over me. I looked at Death, ready to meet my end as he brought out his ginormous laser ax and sliced the head off from 444's body. Tears came down my cheeks. I grabbed my black hair as hard as I could to avoid feeling the current pain of loss. Seconds later, I couldn't move. My body froze over as Death made his way over to me. He was extremely intimidating. I managed to take a step back and tripped on a rock. As I was falling backward, Death, with his ginormous violet laser ax, hacked off my entire left arm. I was screaming in pain, saying, "Just let it end." I surrendered myself to Death, waiting for the final blow.

He walked toward me with his black motorcycle helmet on and said, "Begone, trash." A blazing light appeared out of the sky from space way too luminous to be looked at directly. Both of us were struck in awe. I fell on my butt, and Death looked directly into the light, seeing its enormousness beaming in from space. Massive vibrations could be felt throughout the area. The light was so luminous it was overpowering. Death decided he had seen enough as he ran toward the tower of light. He was immediately obliviated. I sat there now petrified, wondering what the heck was going on. I suddenly felt the pain come back to me from my severed left arm. I began to faint as the light range drew closer to me; the light had a message: "Live!" The light then began to fade back into space. I looked up and screamed, "Why!" The light did not respond as it vanished from the atmosphere. I sat there on my knees for a while until I decided to lie flat on my stomach to recover for a few hours. The pain really started to take over, and the next thing I knew, I blacked out.

XI

Dr. Smart

I WOKE UP AND FOUND myself in a pink room. I was strapped down, not remembering much. Out of fear, I began to scream until I noticed someone had merged me with an entire robotic arm. I looked at my entire robotic shoulder arm stretched out. I was amazed to see how cool it looked on me, and it left like the real thing. For a moment, I began to wish my other arm was severed off as well to make it robotic. Next came the individual who walked through the brown door. I did not know what to say when I saw this faction member standing before me with an all-white coat and a crazy spiral of blue hair reaching to the top of the ceiling. The white coat read "DOCTOR" on one side of his pocket and "SCIENTIST" on the other side of his pocket. His boots seemed to be made out of water, and on one shoulder, he had a clock attached to him and, on the other shoulder, an all-brown tarsier that looked like it was freaking out. He spoke and said, "It's okay, I am a doctor."

I said, "How can I trust you?"

He mentioned, "I could have left you in the crater to die."

I said, "Excuse me? Crater?"

He said, "Yes! The entire City of Earth saw the ginormous beam of light that came from space. It made the whole city tremble. I wasn't too far away at the time, so I decided to check out the commotion. When I got there, I saw you with your injuries and decided to bring you with me before anyone from the city saw you."

I asked him, "What is your name?"

He said in a professional tone, "I am *Dr. Smart*, one of Emperor Fang's former top cabinet members."

"Former top cabinet member?" I asked. "Doctor?"

Smart replied, "Yes! I was relieved of my duties when I decided I no longer wanted to perform experiments on men on the orders of the Last Government. My credentials were stripped from me. I was looked down upon as a fool by the entire faction. My family could not handle the loss of prestige or the embarrassment, so they left me. From that day on, I came to live in the City of Earth, bought this two-story all-glass house, and got into the craft of building old technology like robots or using 3D printers to build humans."

"What!" I said out loud.

"Before the city found out what I was doing and the *Mayor Chunky Ahoy* sent his soldiers to my door one day to destroy what he deemed an abomination. They destroyed the machine, but what they didn't know was that I already knew how to build another one without needing the blueprint. They also were unaware of how many other humans I had already created. What happened next did hurt my heart. The last human I had created using the 3D printer happened to be a man that I came to be best friends with. The human even gave himself a name: *Rich Fruta*! He had brown eyes, black bushy hair, and a long nose. Soldiers stormed into my house, and with a court order, they shoved in my face they took Rich. It was late that night, they took him to the center of the city to behead him with the infamous red laser guillotine. I tried to make my way up the crowds that had assembled. It had been sometime that the city had gotten the opportunity to rally at an event that included the beheading of man. I started punching everyone in my way like a madman. I had to save Rich. He did not deserve this sort of fate. As I continued to make my way to the stage, two big bodies turned around, and both punched me in the eye. I fell straight to the floor and began counting stars. The Mayor Chunky Ahoy had seen me drop to the floor and ordered everyone to beat me down then place me on the stage. They winded up tying me up and throwing me onto the stage with my clothes ripped apart. A really big faction member came over and sat on me to make sure I didn't move. I was told by Mayor Chunky Ahoy to never again get out of line or I would be put down. The mayor began dancing around the stage delighted. He had Rich's head locked in, and the crowd began to holler, 'Let it drop! Let it drop! Let it drop!' I begged they reconsider. I thought of all the fun memories I had created with Rich. I began to wish he had run away like the other humans I had created. At least then he might have lived out his life a little longer, giving him the opportunity to learn how to read like he had wanted. I closed my eyes when the red laser from the guillotine chopped off Rich's head. The mayor picked up his head, tossing it into the crowd, and walked away with a loud applause. From then on, I made sure to keep all the creating ventures as secret as possible, due to the fact I was always being monitored and random inspections would be conducted. I was just happy knowing somewhere out there, a good bunch of humans created from my 3D printer were finding their place in the world outside of my laboratory. I had very high hopes for them. I even had the skin color of their toes turned completely green. The idea was meant to be used as a means of identification. Each member had one toe's skin cells completely altered to display a heavy green skin tone to make sure there was no mistaking it. I created them with the intention they would find a life for themselves. For every life I had taken, I had given one back. I told them to always look out for each other and that they were the *people of the future*.

"Aside from being a doctor, I loved to create, to invent, to enjoy the process of using the creative ability within myself. I also have a knack for the history of the old times. Mankind really had an amazing run at it. Men have been around from quite some time now, but sadly, like all great mass extinctions, things come to an end."

"What do you mean?"

"Well, aside from women also contributing to your numbers, men had begun to outnumber women 10–1, not only on the planet of Rump, but also on the space colonies, including its planetary colonies."

"Wait, so this planet has a name?"

"Yes, it is called Rump, after one of the faction generals that fought in the Space Wars versus man. In the time of man, it used to be called something else, but any record of that information was destroyed by the emperor."

I asked what made the former Faction General *Rump* worth naming an entire planet after. Dr. Smart elaborated Rump, aside the emperor, was the best the faction had to throw at mankind. Rump quickly gained a reputation as he had a giant scar across his forehead from his time as a soldier. His humanoid form put him about six feet tall, and he wore all platinum robes. Rump, at all times, could be seen with a cigar in his mouth. He did not care. He was ruthless. The emperor loved this about rump. His weapon of choice was the *red laser bolo knife*. He became feared quickly. In one of the battles that took place on *Space Colony Four* that he led, it was said no man was able to stop him. On that day he mowed down every man in his path as if he were walking through the jungle, clearing vegetation. Rump made history being the first humanoid faction member to take control over an entire *space colony*. He had delivered a heavy blow to man, taking *Colony Four*. Of all the colonies, it was the one most heavily armed. The conquest of Colony Four marked the beginning of the domino effect for mankind. Rump enslaved every human on that colony, either putting them to work by making them build weapons for the faction army or forcing them to provide food and shelter. In many cases, he would build the other faction members' morale by allowing members to get in bed with the woman. He had live executions of hundreds of men they had captured by letting them loose into the vacuum of space, watching their lifeless bodies float off. Rump was a war genius. He knew existence was given to him for this purpose. One day in a complete public display to everyone in the colony, he took off his platinum robes and, with his red laser bolo knife, cut himself across the chest. He yelled, 'War ready!' There were a lot of humans on board the colonies that wanted a crack at Rump, and he had a very good eye for picking up attention to detail. To avoid a revolt, he set up a stage inside the colony where any human could challenge him one-on-one to a fight. Rump was pretty beefy, and sure enough, many men took his challenges, and each one of them lost their lives. Rump loved violence. He loved fighting. It moved his very core, and his soldiers all loved him for it. The emperor one day arrived at Colony Four and, in private corridors, informed Rump he would be his successor if anything were to ever happen to him. Rump knelt before his emperor and said if this is what he wanted, then so be it.

"I think it is time I unstrap you from the bed so that you can stretch a leg."

Some time passed as Dr. Smart and I spoke for a while, eating our green square meals. Afterward he showed me the laboratory he had built under his home. It was amazing that Dr. Smart had everything you can possibly think about going on down there. He had created a machine he called *Next Level*. With that machine and his brilliant understanding of every form of physics and math ever created, he figured out how to preserve energy of time so that if he wanted to have energy take the form of something with the assistance of nanotechnology, he can literally turn it into whatever his heart desired. Dr. Smart pushed the purple button on the Next Level machine and told me to speak so that the machine could recognize my voice. Afterward he said, "Now request anything you desire."

I had always wanted to fly through the air. I yelled out, "A flying device!"

Dr. Smart started laughing at me, but instantaneously, before my eyes, a fully purple radiating energy that resembled the length of a carpet stood hovering before me. Dr. Smart said, "Stand on the purple energy."

I took a step onto the purple radiating energy, and it merged with my body, outlining a purple aurora. I began to fly around the laboratory freely and asked Smart if I could keep the purple energy. Dr. Smart said he would hold on to it for me and had it turned into a purple pen, which he placed inside one of his pockets.

Dr. Smart was an old-school collector. He had equipment from all ages of mankind. I put on a headset that was lying around. I was amazed by what I was hearing for the first time. From the little screen, it read, "SCHOOLBOY Q 'MAN OF THE YEAR' 2014." I looked around the laboratory and saw something that really caught my attention. I walked over to a huge stasis tube that resembled something along the lines of a cryogenics chamber, and I asked the doctor, "What is this?"

Dr. Smart said, "It is the only *Nano Germ-X* left in existence. I had extracted the sample toward the end of the Space Wars from an infected dying man. Germ-X was one of the many concoctions the faction used in their aid to try and ensure 100 percent annihilation of man. They came to find out that in the end, they came very close, only to discover five hundred men were still left. The emperor wasted no time once the Space War was over, and he created the Dark Faction to hunt down the remaining men. The emperor enjoyed years of being brought to a new man that had been hunted down whose life he could take. The pleasure that he would get from it was similar to someone who was an addict looking for the next high. I am aware that you are only one of four men now left because I, too, had access to a list that I hacked into the system to make a copy of, thinking maybe I could be there to try and save what was left of man. At the end, though, I hesitated, knowing that I, too, had caused so much suffering to so many men. I can see the blood on my hands, and it weighed heavy on me. Under the orders of the Last Government, I was forced in the name of the emperor to see how you guys tickled inside and out. I explored every fabric of your imagination of the human body. At times, I would enhance a human body to see what you guys could do with an upgrade to your DNA code. I am not proud of any of it anyways, for today that is enough. You can stay with me if you would like. I can pass you for one of my more up-to-date human cyborgs, especially with that new fancy arm I merged to your body. I meant to mention I did a tamper with your robe's nano system cells. The black robes are no longer attached to you. I installed a code into your cells that allowed the rejection of those hideous robes. I had a purple robe that I created to merge with your skin cells. To cut a long story short, I also enhanced you by altering your genetic code out of curiosity."

XII

Telepathy

I DECIDED TO FALL ASLEEP in the laboratory; it just felt more like home to me, a collection of relics and new ideas all in one central location. I knew when I saw it, I was going to knock out on this big white roll-out sofa bed. I began to slowly fade away into my mind. As I descended, I saw the darkness I had feared would return from that day in the cave, the Dark Spot once more stalking me like prey. The dark spot stared at me once again with its evil, demonic yellow eyes from before. This time, it chose to attack my mind telepathically; it showed me images of my death. It even spoke to me in my mind. The dark spot said, "This time you shall be mine." I began to see the dark spot shadow, making its way across the lab toward me, getting bigger and bigger. It made it clear to me it had spent its time devouring other life-forms to have gained more strength to ensure it would devour me this time. I lay there tossing and turning. The dark spot, now hovering over me, grabbed me by the arm. I could feel the intense burning where it grabbed me. I begged it to stop, but the dark spot let me know this time I would not escape. I began to scream out for help, "Anybody, please, hear me! Help!" The dark spot touched my lips, and it felt like not only my mouth had been sealed shut, but my mouth was also on fire. At one point it, hit me like a hard thump on my head.

I could hear a voice saying, "Who is this?" It took me a good second to really piece it together, for I had never heard this voice before, and yet again it said, "Who is this?"

I came more to my senses. I realized it was the voice of another man. I asked, "Can you hear me?"

The voice, in a bewildered tone, said, "Yes," and then an awkward pause took place for several minutes. In that moment, the dark spot retreated, letting me know the third time will be the charm.

The man's voice said, "Where are you?"

I hesitantly replied for the fear of slowly seeing those evil, demonic yellow eyes fade. "Right here!"

The voice said, "Right here where?"

It was at that moment that I realized somehow my mind connected with that of another man. I said out loud, "My name is 23. What is your name?"

For a good while, there was no answer, and finally, with some confidence, the man said, "My name is 371."

My jaw dropped in amazement. I asked, "So you're alive!"

371 said, "Yes, why wouldn't I be?"

From that moment on, we were both on the same track. 371 mentioned that there still lived two other men, 99 and 311.

What 371 brought to my attention was that our fellow humans from the Space Wars left us with an option on how we can ensure that mankind carries on. I would have to find a way into the ancient city of man that lay under the City of Earth. Once I found the underground city, I needed to locate an all-white building that would have a giant gold crest in the front of the building. In that building I would find answers. 371 mentioned to be careful; wild abominations, once men who were experimented on by a renowned faction doctor, roamed the ruined city, and they are nothing to take lightly. The Last Government knew about the ruined cities to ensure that no one ever decided to venture off. They released all the men they had experimented on that they had turned into abominations into the ruined cities of man.

I informed 371, "Thanks for the heads-up." I also asked 371, "Where exactly are you?"

He responded, "That is something you need not know, in case they happen to be listening to us."

I never took that into consideration. At that moment, the connection was lost. I woke up in a deep sweat, wondering what the heck had happened. I was beginning to think I lost my mind, when I looked at my arm and saw the burn mark from the dark spot on me.

I had decided to touch the burn mark and immediately felt the pain shoot through my body. I touched my mouth and felt the burn to my lips. I was pretty terrified. I was not ready for what came next. A black shadowlike spike went through my leg. I heard a familiar voice speak into my ear; it was the dark spot. It had taken a woman's voice and said how it was going to enjoy devouring me like a blob; it pounced on me. I hit the floor and noticed this time the dark spot was too much for me. The dark spot mentioned how it enjoyed me playing in its dark-yellow yolk sometime ago. It loved how I had made love to it and now was going to extract every ounce of energy that existed within my body until I ceased to exist. I felt it happening quickly. The nutrients from my body were indeed being extracted, and I felt myself aging. This thing was not playing, and it had me pinned down. It said to me I should be proud that an entity from another dimension had taken its interest in devouring me. I tried to yell for help, but nothing worked; this was the end.

In that second, one of Dr. Smart's androids had come into the laboratory and turned on all the lights. The dark spot could not handle the light and quickly made for whatever shadows it could find. I saw it had run under a lab table. I had decided I was going to at least find a way to contain this thing here and now while it was at a disadvantage. I looked around the laboratory and found a device that read "vacuum"; this had a tube chamber about the size of a water bottle. I picked the device and held it in my hand like a gun and went to the lab table where the dark spot resided under. I let the dark spot know it was my time to show it what a little fear felt like. The dark spot yelled at me, telling me to stay away from it. I turned the vacuum on, and it made all kinds of crazy noises. I could hear it powering up. There was a button that read Extract, which I pushed. What I saw next was something that looked like gravitational waves.

These waves began to extract the dark spot from under the table. It began cursing a storm at me, telling me how dare I do this. The dark spot was extracted and filled the chamber contained in the vacuum. I turned the device off and placed it on the far corner of the lab by some other crazy inventions Dr. Smart had lying around. I could see the demonic yellow eyes looking at me from inside the chamber now with such hatred that I simply said, "This is your doing," and walked away with a smile.

I walked up to the android and asked what its name was. It said, "My name is *Bingo*."

I said, "Well, Bingo, I owe you a drink. You saved my life."

Bingo said he had not drunk since he saw the former android *Roy* become an alcoholic and wear his parts down until he fell apart. I asked Bingo what he does around here. Bingo mentioned he cleans the house and he keeps the laboratory up-to-date. He continued to elaborate how he was created to protect Dr. Smart as his sole body-guard. He cooks for Dr. Smart, and he has his clothes ready for him and makes sure he has all the latest information for him. I said, "Then you're kinda like the butler for Dr. Smart?" Bingo looked at me with a certain stare. I noticed he had an eyeglass on his left eye, including a black-and-white tailored suit on. I asked Bingo if he also enjoys working with Dr. Smart. Bingo mentioned a time when he went with Dr. Smart to the icy oceans of the southern region of UNO and discovered some penguin fossils. They extracted the fossils from the ground and took them to the mini laboratories they had set up. Within a matter of hours, they had these penguins that had not existed in forever running around in the hundreds.

The far southern region of Rump is completely covered over in ice. The far northern region is also covered over in ice, yet the faction had used their highly advanced technology to allow them to survive and live anywhere on the planet Rump. While we were hundreds of miles away from the nearest city, being the Faction City of Mars, plenty of faction members had made their homes along the way down to the frozen oceans. A lot of the beauty still remained under the city. Dr. Smart one day had drilled a hole into the ice. He sent down nanospiders that gave us a screen view of what was going on under the ice. What Dr. Smart discovered there were all kinds of species thriving under the ice. He was excited and wanted to share the news with the world, but he knew his fellow faction members would come and destroy a good thing from all the visitors. I have enjoyed the many off-the-wall creations and ideas Dr. Smart has explored. It was sad to see his wife leave him and his daughter. They mean so much to him. He will never admit it, but at night, he smokes himself to sleep. There are a lot of memories that haunt him. When he begins to show signs of depression, it is my job to cheer him up and bring him back to reality. That's how a lot of his backyard projects started, with him adding a garden with fruit trees. When he is outside, I ensure he has a pen and paper, for he is always lost in thought. Dr. Smart is a full-time job these days, and without me, I worry he would not shower or eat. There were days he would just spend his time reading. I would keep myself busy by picking up a new craft. I feel my responsibility is to continue to learn as much as possible. Right now I just completed my training in architecture, construction management, and engineering. I have built some pretty amazing homes in the city. Last month I was awarded the *Outstanding Award* for designing and having built ten of my most prestigious house designs.

Bingo has really enjoyed traveling throughout the vastness of Uno with Dr. Smart; he has even enjoyed the journeys through space with him. He noted some of the views that exist in space are simply to die for. One thing Bingo recalls vividly was when he came into existence and the first thing he saw was Dr. Smart at that time with his gold glasses and hearty smile. He had a cup of coffee in his hands, which he had dropped from excitement. I caught the cup in midair and took a sip from; I was amazed such a delicious beverage existed. I then realized I could smell all kinds of things.

XIII

Colossus

DR. SMART CAME INTO THE lab asking if everything was alright. He mentioned he saw last night's feed from the video cameras and noticed some funny business. I told him that I need to know the entrance to the hidden ruined city below us. Dr. Smart mentioned that the city has been gone for some time now. I told him there had to be a way. I let Dr. Smart know I was seeking information. Dr. Smart went on to say, "Well, the city is only lost if you don't know how to look."

I asked, "What do you mean?"

He began to walk then looked back at me and told me to walk with him. We walked over to an area of his lab where he had many work desks covered in blueprints. I saw what looked like a board game and asked Dr. Smart about it. He explained that it was a chessboard and he is the current world chess champion on Rump. I was pretty amazed at the beauty and quality of the board and its unique pieces.

Dr. Smart mentioned, "Chess is a game that originated in man's ancient times and has managed to survive through what they called the BC times, AD times, and now GT times."

I asked, "What does 'GT times' mean?"

Dr. Smart answered, "It stands for 'Galactic Times.' This planet has been around now for such a long time. Like I mentioned before, it has gone through several name changes due to the inhabitants that have come and gone. We are at the point now where our sun could go red giant and we would be forced to relocate off Rump."

I asked the question, "Then what?"

"Well, that is a question for another time. The only reason we continue to be alive is through the superior advances in technology the faction has created. The faction made this planet a new ozone layer. They even managed to create another version of water, in case it ever dried out on us again. There is just about nothing the faction can't create. They are the product and embodiment of supergenius. Their minds are infused with nanotechnology that allows that to process at levels above supercomputers—the smart ones, that is."

Dr. Smart mentioned, "I am amongst the top three smartest faction members alive today. While the faction has made changes to improve Rump, there are things they also have not managed to overturn. This planet remains at a chill, never truly able to gain enough heat to get over fifty degrees again. The planet remains in a dark, shadowy form from space due to the countless years of destruction to the very composition of this planet. When man started sending bigger spacecraft to outer space to help build the space colonies, the amount of fuel waste the crafts would emit would leave a permanent black lingering slush in the atmosphere. At that time, the planet already lost all vegetation. The faction managed to engineer those mini green square meals we all eat to feed the current inhabitants. This planet is truly a resilient one. She continues to withstand all that we do to her. While with the Last Government, I was forced to create a power source that would keep Rump's inner liquid core moving, preventing it from coming to a halt. I had developed a way to extract all the radioactive elements that resided at the planet's core to later create into a power source that would allow for more fuel efficient spacecraft. I even won the Nobel Peace Prize for being the first humanoid faction member to create the capability of traveling at the speed of light, something that did not exist during the Space Wars era. The spacecraft in that time period were efficient in travel, but the technology had not existed yet to be able to travel at the speed of light. With the help of nanotechnology and the material and minerals I discovered on other planets, I hit a breakthrough one night in this very laboratory.

"I have found what I wanted to show you. This thing is called a nanoportal. It can transport you to anywhere your mind wants to go, even if you have never been there before. It will lock in with your brain's neurotransmitters to link in with one of the mega satellites in space. You use the satellite GPS to find your desired location. The nanoportal was the size of a mini tablet, and once your location is located, it will teleport your body over. To start, all you need to do is inform the device to merge, and it will warp into your brain. It connects inside of your mind as if it were just another part of your brain operating as one."

I yelled, "MERGE!" And before I knew it, everything went white, next dark all in a matter of seconds, and then I found myself in a whole new location. I looked around, and I was standing on a hill. I saw a colossal city in the distance. I shouldn't have spoken so loud because I still had questions for Dr. Smart.

The device said, "Aside this jump, you have one jump left. Thank you for traveling with *Air Super*. We hope you enjoyed your ride. Please fly again with us soon. If you visit our website, you will see that we have specials with low rates guaranteed! Anytime you're looking to travel, either to the space colonies or any planetary colony. Thank you and have a great day."

I made my way down to the ruined city. The word *colossal* is an understatement. It looked like someone had nuked the city and left it for dead.

I made my way into the city, and the stench of death embodied my surroundings. I had to be careful at every step because every few seconds, something was collapsing around me. It was harder to navigate because of the heavy darkness that loomed over the area; it felt as though I was at a graveyard. I walked forward. My stomach began to turn, and the hairs on the back of my neck stood tall. Something about this place just felt off. What was left of the building structures appeared to even have a black streak going across them. There were parts of the colossal city that sank further into the ground. What appeared were skyscrapers lying next to one another leveled as if they were coffins. Thankfully, due to the enhancements from Dr. Smart, I was able to climb over monuments and get around in a way I was never able to before. I was amazed because I was never in my life capable of even climbing a medium-size dead tree. At one point, I was surprised how I no longer had to worry about stamina. I was climbing up, halfway up a human statue, and realized that I had been climbing over this head for an hour now. One wrong grip and I would fall to my death. I really did not know where I was going, but in my mind, I knew that as long as I kept going forward, I would find the all-white building with the golden emblem at the front of it. I quickly came to realize I could also run without getting tired, which made this process a lot easier; I was able to make giant leaps, which was pretty fascinating in itself. I was running so fast, and it was so dark that I felt from my last step that there was absolutely nothing below me. It wasn't until I reached the other side that I realized what I had done. I turned around and saw there must have been a massive quake or massive sinkhole because there was nothing. I felt discouraged that this wasn't panning out the way I had envisioned it. There was no telling how much of a dent I have even made or if the building even still existed due to the terrain shifting or even just time. I was trying hard to keep my hopes up.

After what felt like a day pass by, I was done. Maybe if I go back to Dr. Smart, then he would have an idea. He is really good with looking at things in depth. Next thing I knew, something grabbed me from behind and, with such force, slammed me to the ground. I was seeing stars in every direction from the sheer force of the slam. It was so heavy I could hear a yelling sound coming from what I could only imagine was one of the abominations. I couldn't get the thing off me. It pierced my back with one of its claws. I felt my flesh being sliced, and it began to pound on my back with such massive force that the only reason I am alive, I am sure, is due to the enhancements by Dr. Smart. It felt like I was only absorbing a quarter of the force of its blows. I tried to lift it with my cool robotic hand, but this abomination was so heavy it felt like a tower was on my back. I was starting to panic because I was running out of options quickly. With the final massive blow the abomination gave me, it made the ground around us collapse. We fell through the street in what felt like a good ten seconds. We landed on something heavy because I could see the abomination had splattered all over. The dust began to settle a bit, and I noticed that not only did we land in the middle of a gold emblem, but it was the white building I had been looking for.

I made myself into the building, and part of it was smashed in with my upgrade in strength. I was able to move aside rubble, and I made my way farther into the building. I quickly noticed this used to be some sort of research center. I walked into several rooms and saw cryochambers and chemicals laid out for someone within the chemistry field. I made my way down the big hall on the wall. I could see a sign that read "The Main Laboratory Straight Ahead" and another one that read "Golden Star Chamber to the right." I arrived at the laboratory, and the two doors were locked. I decided I'd lean into the doors, forcing my way in, and after several loud thumps, I managed to burst my way in. Once inside, I saw a giant supercomputer that took up an entire wall. With one giant screen, it looked like it was built to withstand some heavy-duty situations. The eternity of the machine was in mint condition. As I took my fifth step, the lights turned on. The supercomputer made a very loud start-up noise. A heavy steel door behind me slid down and locked me in. I walked closer to the supercomputer. I saw a wireless keyboard laid out. It hadn't been more than a few minutes when I heard loud, thunderous blows pounding on the steel door. I figured the loud noise from the supercomputer must have gotten the attention of the abominations that must have been nearby. I focused my eyes back on the giant screen and tried to block out the massive thumps to the steel door. I knew time was of the essence. I noticed on the screen it said YES or No. Unsure, I hit the YES button, thinking maybe some sort of details or files would populate on the big screen. The next thing on the big screen struck fear into me. A timer started one minute and counting. Information popped up on the screen, saying, "You have initiated YES to activate the *black hole weapon*. This weapon, upon igniting, will consume this city, and the City of Earth man will survive." A video this time popped up on the big screen of what looked like a high-ranking soldier with a Golden Star on his chest.

He said, "Man will reclaim what is theirs. Thank you, *Mr. President*, and may the *Space Wars* end in our favor." I began something that I could not stop with fifteen seconds left on the timer. I had to quickly think of where I would teleport. Without thinking of what was happening at the door, another abomination grabbed me, piercing me straight through my ribs. Another abomination bit the side of my neck and tore a piece of skin off. I didn't have time to yell since the computer screen read, "One second." I was able to see through my peripherals that at least five abominations were in the rooming now fighting among one another to get a piece of me. I thought of a place, and all I remember is feeling the force of something truly massive pass through my body. The upgrade saved me because while my body wasn't destroyed, all the abominations in the room from the shock wave force were ripped apart. A split second later, I was transported.

XIV

Decimation

I AM NOT SURE WHY it was on my mind, but I found myself in the City of Taste, the capital of where the emperor resided within his golden palace. I was still bleeding from my wounds, including the damage to my ribs I took from the abomination. I had to find a doctor. I began to make my way around, asking desperately if someone knew where I could find a doctor. I didn't realize that everyone around me was in a panic as well, so I looked over to what appeared to be a restaurant named *El Grande Tacos* and saw a nanoprojector that created a hologram of City of Earth. From the images being projected, it would appear that the *black hole weapon* not only sucked the two cities in but also took a chunk of the western part of the supercontinent. The news was calling it a *terrorist attack* by man. I was responsible for all the lives that I took in that moment, but I did not feel the least guilty for whatever reason. What I wanted was to find a doctor until it dawned on me that Dr. Smart was gone too. I shed a few tears for Dr. Smart and began to make my way into the city. I saw a half-drunk bottle of *holy shmoly tequila* lying on the ground by a dumpster. I decided that, aside from not having a doctor around, the next best thing was a drink of tequila, so I decided to get pretty tipsy to allow the pain to subside a bit. I was quickly spotted by a few soldiers lying half passed out at the side of a dumpster. I immediately began to run, and within minutes, I had a whole squadron chasing me down. I knew I had to find somewhere to hide due to the amount of blood I was losing, having made things worse by thinning out my blood from the delicious tequila. I did not know the way around this city. I just decided to run in any direction or alleyway where a soldier was not present, falling over multiple trash cans in the process. With one wrong turn, a soldier hit me in the head with the butt of his laser rifle. I fell to the ground as I began to black out, and all that I could remember hearing was laser fire coming from multiple directions.

I woke up and found myself strapped down to a table that was made from pure energy, radiating a very bright orange aura. This time a mini orange laser blade was at my throat. My eyes were blurry coming back into perspective. I had a giant light on me, and to the side of me, I noticed several tools of pain laid out on counters. I scanned the room, only to see it filled with gangbangers, thugs, hit men, bounty hunters, and ex-soldiers. One of them stood out to me as a pure nutjob. He was wearing an all-white suit with a white mask on, and a blue X painted across the white mask, including the fact he also had a bazooka attached to his chest. The bazooka must have been customized, made and designed by a talented artist, because it had an image of a tank shooting at an entire planet and the planet exploding. I truly got the sense of this character being a bit off.

A woman approached me out of the shadows covered in tattoos with a pure-red Mohawk, scars all over her brown-skinned body, with a pair of red boots that came all the way up to her waist. She didn't wear her robes. What she had on was a red woman's bra with a black pair of ripped jean shorts. She demanded to know who I was or she would have the mini laser slowly slice my throat. The situation did not look good, and telling from the look on her face, she meant business. Without having much of a choice, I informed her my name is 23.

Immediately the dark room began to whisper as she said, "You are a man." She approached me even closer and began to lick the side of my neck with her tattooed tongue; she said, "You are indeed a man and one that might make me a rich woman. I am a former alpha to the enforcers. They call me *Sage Roja* around here, leader of the *Bandits*, former misfits to the Last Government. Luckily for you, 23, we no longer serve the Last Government ever since they betrayed us in a weapons deal gone bad. What I do want to know is how valuable you are, for currency goes a long way." Sage used the nanotechnology that she had merged into her wrist to project a hologram of a direct call she was making to Emperor Fang.

At that moment, a tall figure was projected, and the emperor took his place in the room. Sage bowed along with everyone else and mentioned she had a gift. The emperor immediately placed his eyes on me and said I must be the one who committed the terrorist attack. The emperor demanded answers, and when I remained silent, he yelled at Sage to make me talk. She took out of her pocket mini nanodrones, which flew into the air through my nose and latched onto my brain to project all my memories. The emperor saw it all and was enraged! He demanded that I be brought to his palace immediately, which was when Sage asked what the pay would be.

The emperor noted there was to be no pay. "What you will receive in payment is keeping your lives."

Sage yelled that was not good enough. The emperor mentioned what a shame he had already locked into her location.

A giant explosion took place that left rubble everywhere, including on top of me. I began to see laser shots going in every direction, and another member of the Dark Faction appeared. I knew who this was from 444's stories. It was *Sin*. His signature weapon was using a green laser whip; he would make quick work of the bodies around him. As Sin approached me, I saw he wore an all-green robe. His face was all black, and he had long green hair that dragged on the ground like a roll-out carpet. Anyone who stood before him as he walked toward me quickly met their end; he quickly piled up his body count so that you could see the carnage he had implemented all around him. He finally reached me and used his green laser whip to free me; he then punched me straight in the face. I began to see all kinds of green stars. All I remember is being picked up by Sin, who began making his way to the exit, when he fell to one knee. I could hear the anger boiling inside him. From behind, Sage hit him with a laser spear that tore through his right pectoral. I hit the ground, and he punched me square in the face again to knock me out, he stood up and he pulled out his green laser whip. SAGE pulled out her yellow laser bagh nakh. The two went tick for tack in an equal fight. The area around us became unstable, and both sides began to take casualties.

As I lay on the ground, I saw it all play out. Whoever was in the all white suit with the white mask on that had a blue X on it just let loose on his bazooka fire. He was running around like a madman killing many faction soldiers. This Character X was like a game pro making the perfect jump when needed, finding the right location with a clear vantage point. His kill streak was complete madness within a matter of minutes. I slid myself under a pool table, scared I might get caught in the cross fire. I saw Character X running around, laughing in madness, as a soldier came close to stabbing him, when he knocked him out with his bazooka fire, hitting him straight in the head.

From the crumbling ceiling came another individual dressed in an all-black suit wearing a black mask with a yellow X across the mask, holding in his hands a detonator. He pushed it, and a massive explosion went off outside. I could hear screaming. The force from the explosion was so strong that the whole place shook. From what I gathered, I was inside a huge bricked warehouse. The number of bodies that were piling up provided me with great cover as if multiple layers of sandbags had been placed before me to protect me. There seemed to be no end to the faction soldiers storming in. You could easily make them out with their shining bronze helmets, their bronze robes with bronze tactical boots, and their standard laser gun at one side of the hip, standard laser mini sword on the other, and on their back, a standard laser shield. Their faces were completely covered by a bronze war mask. I had heard stories from 444 that each soldier in the faction went through rigorous training, and at the end, they had to show they had the balls to take the life of someone they knew before they could be pledged in. A tall soldier made his way into the area with several other soldiers at his side; a few bandits had caught them by surprise, and a full battle royal took place until Character X shot his now-two bazooka shots in their direction, completely killing them all in sight. A giant tank made its way into the facility and ran over the character with the all-black suit and black mask with a yellow X on it. Character X saw this and began his rapid bazooka fire on the tank. The next thing I heard was a massive shot from the tank fire and the shell going straight through Character X, obliterating everything in sight. Several other bandits had thrown some grenades inside the tank, killing whoever was inside.

The carnage was on another level. Two helicopters came into sight, blasting at everything they saw that was not wearing bronze; blood quickly covered the entire area. I attempted to make my way out, but I was feeling weak from my injuries. I looked around to see if Sage and Sin were still exchanging blows. I quickly spotted them. Each of their weapons, upon collision, sent sparks flying from the impacts. Both had been damaged, but around them, bodies were piled to the point they were fighting on top of bodies. As the two continued to fight, they each had opposing enemies confront them during their battle. A few other bandits had shot down both helicopters, and one came crashing down onto the building, while the other exploded next to Sin, sending him flying against the bricked wall. When he stood up, his green robes had been melted off from the explosion. He had taken heavy damage. His weapon had been lost in the explosion, and one of his legs appeared to be broken. Sage, with her superior speed, made her way to Sin and ruptured his head with the blows she delivered to him from her yellow laser bagh nakh. Afterward several soldiers made their way toward her, one of them grabbing her and ramming her through a brick wall. The soldier walked right up to her and was going to take her head with his laser sword, when she quickly picked up a laser gun beside her and shot him in the face. She stumbled to the ground, and you could see an expression on her face that showed the lights were on but no one was home. She was moving on pure instinct. Sage made her way over to me. She attempted to grab me when one of the soldiers put a laser blade through her kidney. She pulled out the mini laser knife she had in her back short pocket and stabbed the soldier through the throat. She walked toward me again, and another soldier came up to her and stabbed her in the stomach. She drove her knife through his eye. She made her way toward me again, and this time, a soldier had stabbed her straight through the heart. She fell to the ground, and her red eyes faded away. A handful of soldiers grabbed me from under the pool table and began their exit out of the facility. Along the way, many of the soldiers dropped from the laser fire. The soldiers were aware of the importance of making sure they delivered me to the emperor. They tightened their formation, and as they made their way out, it was a complete masterpiece of death. This is what they had trained for. They would all be highly rewarded and recognized by the emperor. When the last soldier was out, they hit the neon-orange button to a detonator, and a massive explosion followed, completely laying waste to the massive warehouse.

I found myself in a military vehicle, being transported by a soldier driving and a soldier holding a laser gun to my stomach. They were cheering, saying the emperor was surely going to recognize their efforts; they would probably even get promoted. The one holding the gun to me said, "The emperor truly wants you, to have sent such a militia in to retrieve you. Think of yourself lucky it has been a while since the emperor went to these measures."

The driver said, "I have waited years to get promoted from lieutenant to captain. All that time driving around bored, blasting nomads in the middle of the night to kill some time is finally paying off." The driver mentioned how his wife might even finally make love to him again. She was a human woman who was attracted to humanoid faction members. They had met at a party, and the rest was history. He mentioned how everything was great until she started finding him boring. She had loved he was a man in a uniform but would only give it up to him when he would get promoted, so he was long overdue.

The soldier holding the gun said he enjoyed the company of other male humanoids. He wasn't attracted to women. He had an entourage, and with his promotion to captain, he would go to the City of V with them and find where the party scene nightlife was to celebrate.

The driver brought out a flask and said, "Why wait to celebrate when you can start now?"

They both started getting loaded and started to get rowdy. The one holding the gun lowered the window and started blasting everything that came into sight. The driver began to severe so much they received a radio call from the other military truck following from behind, asking if everything was alright.

The driver answered, "Everything is good here, just a nanospider in the cab."

XV

Emperor Hola

I WOKE UP KNEELING BEFORE the emperor; they had nanoweights that hovered over me, creating a type of gravity to hold me down. I had no way of moving. For the first time, I came face-to-face with *Emperor Fang Hola*. He was truly a tall humanoid, approximately eight feet tall; his entire body was built like a massive bodybuilder. I could see why his own faction members and soldiers feared him; he had a bald head full of tattoos, and his robes were pure gold weighted at two hundred pounds. The emperor started by saying, "I know that you are the one they call 23. I also know that I was the one who drove my *purple Haladie laser* through your father's heart, Mr. 22. After the nukes went off, a massive energy of light beamed down with about five hundred men, according to our intel. Your father was leading the pack. Mr. 22 was considered a very high-priority asset to us due to the fact he was the captain of all ten space colonies. The faction had already figured that man must have had a few contingency plans in case anything ever happened to them, for your species just doesn't know when to quit. Once we extracted all the information that we could from your father's brain cells, I took him to the front of my palace so that all could see. We broadcasted it live for the men who had escaped to see. I drove my purple Haladie laser through his heart. I saw the life leave his brown eyes. I kicked his lifeless body down the stairs, and everyone cheered. I created the Dark Faction to destroy every man found but, at the same time, to extract every bit of DNA code from each and every man, because your father, Mr. 22, hid the codes to the *Angel devastator*, also known as *angel* inside one of you. I know for a fact the angel aided you when combating Death. Each one of my faction members have a nanovideo installed in their thoughts. The reason I have not been able to find the angel is because its creator managed to create it out of a material that allows it to camouflage with outer space. That weapon has the power to destroy entire planets. At full power with codes inserted, it truly becomes an angel of death. The angel at max power cannot only explode a star but has the sheer power to awaken the galaxy black hole to start its consumption of everything around it. It was one of man's last options as a means of ensuring that the faction did not claim victory over the Space Wars, but at the end, man was too soft to push the blue button. When I saw the video, it became clear to me that a lone survivor must be operating the angel because the group of men who stole one of my army's ships years ago. We detonated the ship from my palace. Every one of our machines and aircraft not only has a tracking device but also a detention device for security purposes. How surprised they must have all been when they reached outer space just to be destroyed."

I was sick to my stomach from everything that the emperor told me. The emperor then proceeded with the words "stand up," as the confinement forced gravity made me stand. The emperor had them bring him some all-white gloves. When he put them on the tops of his fingers, they began radiating with what looked like a mini red laser on the tip of each finger. He asked me, "Do you know what is going to come next?"

I said, "*No.* I do not."

The emperor smiled in delight and said, "Pain. A lot of pain. I am going to extract from your very core every ounce of your existence with the assistance of my *nano-piranha bots* until I get codes to the angel." A big pan was put in front of me, and Emperor Hola mentioned things were about to get messy. Emperor Hola thrust his fingers into me. I immediately felt the tips of the laser from his fingertips cut through me, and I felt the terrible biting from the nano-piranha bots tearing up my insides as well as collecting my genetic data. I was screaming in pain, and every time he took his fingers out of my guts, my blood would fall into the pan. I can feel myself being internally destroyed literally from the inside out. I could not manage this pain for long. I actually may die from this. I began to see the room go from white and transition into darkness. With his buff hands, he continued to let me have it, distracted in his play of administering me pain.

We both heard the heads from the guards in the room hit the floor. Out the shadow two figures appeared, one with a *brown laser katana* and another with a *white bow-and-arrow laser*. The emperor said, "About time, gentlemen. 99 and 311, where have you been hiding all this time? My Dark Faction informed me on several occasions how difficult it was to track you two." It was unfair still how big the emperor was over 99 as he looked directly at the emperor with his brown laser katana. He said, "Leave 23 alone. He is not the one with the codes." The emperor then demanded to know who had them.

99 said, "I do. Mr. 22 entrusted me, his right-hand man, with the codes." At that moment, the emperor lunged forward at 99 with his purple Haladie laser. He wound up taking a direct shot from 311's white laser bow and arrow through the right pectoral. The emperor was so determined that he used his brute force to weather the blow and engaged in full combat with 99. That allowed 311 to come free me; he healed my wounds with what appeared to be nanoclay that merged with my body to replace what was lost. We could hear more soldiers coming to aid the emperor as we were running out of time. 311 made the choice to lead us out down the stairwell.

I asked him, "What about 99?"

He said, "He is not as important as you, 23. You indeed do carry the codes to Angel." I did not find that comforting to know. I looked at him with a surprised expression, not knowing what to say to all the newly acquired information, let alone finding all this out from a complete stranger.

311 said, "The code lies in your number, 23, not in the DNA. We were all branded to try and throw off the faction. One of the ways you can gain access to the codes is by extracting them with a *nanomosquito*. It will extract the code straight from the 23 brand on your skin."

It was a marvelous fight, one year in the making. The emperor had waited so long for a worthy fighter since killing Mr. 22, and now he has the next best thing, his trusted right-hand man, 99. 99 made it clear that the emperor was nothing compared to Mr. 22; he was a true leader. Emperor Hola smiled in delight and said that what his wife said as I had my top scientist Dr. Smart torture her and experiment on her. I truly believed she had the codes. I figured of all people, he would entrust his wife with such information. So, I had Dr. Smart get deep into her in every imaginable way. There were days and nights I could hear her screaming, and it brought me such joy knowing that the possible next president to your stupid Republic was hollering for death down my halls. When it became clear that she did not possess the codes, I had Dr. Smart turn her into an abomination and tossed her down to one of the ruined cities. It is truly poetic, for such a woman of her caliber, prestige, and beauty to be turned into an abomination, a mindless beast with the power to tear anything apart. Those abominations are exactly that massive figures the size of rhinos, their insides turned inside out, fused with whatever was in their surroundings at the time. I actually recall the whole thing now; we had placed Mrs. 22 in a faction bio-engineered jungle when we had her turn. The end result was a monstrosity covered in piercing horns blanketed completely in mud. The final ticker was when I ordered my soldiers to board her up in a cage and fly her over in a cargo ship to dump her into a man ruined city, under the City of Earth, and exploded the entrance to ensure no one inside could ever escape the darkness.

The emperor was very skilled at playing mind games with his opponents. His story had shifted the confidence 99 had to one more now of a heavy heart. 99 felt responsible for the capture of his friend and his wife. That is when the emperor stepped it up and began delivering bigger blows with his purple Haladie laser. 99 had a beautiful brown katana and, like Mr. 22 he was skilled in many forms of combat. The two fought throughout the entire chamber sparks from their impacts flying everywhere. 99 had one good eye and one made from nano-technology as they fought he projected from his nano-eye, a scene where Dr. Smart searched the supercontinent for both

99 and 311. It showed how Dr. Smart provided intel to the both of them, about the whereabouts of 23, and how to get into the emperor's palace. It even provided them each with their laser weapons. The hologram ended, and this enraged the emperor even more. "That traitor Dr. Smart." The fight picked up, and 99 had managed to land a blow on the emperor's left arm. At this point, Emperor Fang snapped and went into his bloodlust mode, and the fight led to one of the palace's balconies. The emperor, you could see his eyes had turned red; he was now driven by pure thirst for blood. His purple Haladie had made multiple cuts across 99's body. He quickly followed with another sequence of combinations that dropped 99 to his knees, blood dripping from his entire body; the end was near now. The victor picked up the brown laser katana and asked if 99 had any finals words. 99 mentioned, "Mankind will defeat the faction!" And with that, Emperor Hola sliced off 99's head with the brown laser katana. In that moment, such bliss passed through the emperor that caused his arousal to very high levels that he wanted more.

At that moment, the head of 99 was thrown in front of us. Emperor Hola looked at us and jumped down from the balcony of his golden palace in his entire mightiness, landing like a tank. He had us surrounded, nowhere left to go. In raw power, he ripped his gold robes off his chest, as he appeared to grow bigger in size, as he flexed his enormous muscles. Every step he took made a dent into the ground the soldiers that surrounded us began a battle cry. 311 looked at me and made it clear there is no way out; all that is left is to confront the emperor. 311 threw his white laser bow and arrow to the ground. he tore his shirt off in rage. The two ran at each other, 311 having to rely on his speed with his smaller frame. One good direct punch from Emperor Hola would be enough to put 311 down. I witnessed the fight carry on. I looked around and saw every soldier's face. I looked up to the heavens, and it dawned on me. Perhaps I could use my telepathy to get in contact with 371. I closed my eyes and tried my hardest to connect my mind. I closed out the noise, and slowly as if the switch turned on, I could sense I had connected.

I said, "371!"

A voice said, "What do you want?"

I mentioned, "We need help. I know that it was you on Angel." He silenced himself for a minute, surprised by the information. I told him that, "I discovered that my father was Mr. 22, and he put the codes for Angel inside of my 23 brand, but right now Emperor Hola was trying to take them." I felt something had splat across my face, I opened my eyes, and I saw that Emperor Hola was making quick work of 311. He had one eye closed, all his teeth were knocked out, and his body looked beat down.

I closed my eyes and told 371, "We are out of time. We need help right now!" Within seconds, I hear this roar come from space. This massive amount of energy hits the center of the city.

371 mentioned, "To avoid the emperor from getting the codes, I am going to level the city." The final thing 371 said was, "You probably have about three minutes, max, before you're completely wiped from the supercontinent Uno." The entire city began to tremble; structures began to get ripped from the ground and tossed around in what looked like a supertornado. Faction members started to make a run for their lives as everyone started freaking out. The emperor, after making sure to pound 311's skull in, told his soldiers, "Do whatever it takes to lock in to the Angel. This is the opportunity of a lifetime, let's make it count." The ground around us began to have massive waves of tremors; the emperor looked at me and, with a smile, turned away. I had the feeling that his current desire was the location of the Angel; nothing else mattered at the moment.

I had to find cover, so I ran over to a building nearby, kicked the door down, and ran down to the basement, where a few other faction members were hiding. I closed my eyes and desperately wanted to see what was going on. I was able to see from the eyes of the emperor he was in his war room with his other generals looking on the big screens they had located the Angel. They had a few ships of their own in space shooting at it aside from the red laser cannon being fired from Rump. The emperor, at the top of his lungs, was screaming to only disable it. The beam intensified, and I could see from his eyes before him the City of Taste being wiped away. Parts of the land had even collapsed as the beam widened in range, I could hear the emperor yell, "This is it!" Lava emerged from the ground, eating away part of the city, you can hear faction members screaming in pain for help, others yelling, "This is the end," then there was silence. I could see that the emperor was displeased he had managed to disarm the ANGEL, but it also managed to destroy the ships attacking it. The Angel had been damaged and could not go back into camouflage mode; it would only be a matter of time now before the Angel was in the hands of Emperor Hola.

XVI

Intelligent Design

THE BASEMENT THAT I WAS hiding in collapsed into the planet from the sheer force of the Angel. I knew whatever happened at the surface could not be good as I stood up in a dark tunnel. Looking around, I saw one surviving faction member rise to their feet. They immediately said, "You are the one that all of this commotion is about!" I stared at them with a blank face. I turned around and began to walk away. I was not going to stop. I had been through a lot, and the last thing I need was someone making me feel guilty.

The voice said, "*Stop!* Where are you going?"

I replied, "Anywhere but here."

The voice said, "I can guide you."

I looked back and said, "What is your name?"

The voice answered, "They call me *Bell Maga*, and I am amongst the top ten smartest faction prodigies."

I said, "Is that right! Then where are we, smart one?"

Bell Maga went on to say, "According to these tunnels and the purple gems glowing from the walls, we just happened to stumble upon one of the underground systems women used."

"What do you mean the underground system that women used?"

"When the faction started mating with women, there was actually a big group of women who did not want to participate. The faction started beheading the women who did not want to mate. The emperor even had his Alpha Enforcer ensure women came to understand the sense of the word *loyalty*. So over time women did what the emperor was trying to avoid. They formed their own resistance called *the Resistance of Eve*. The power of the Last Government was too strong. The resistance decided that they would head underground and create a tunnel system that only they knew. A good chunk of women left to the tunnels, and over time, they were forgotten about. Those women ensured they would not be found. What was also noted later was that they stole some technology from the faction, but it was never broadcasted to the public what that was."

We decided to walk forward following the glow from the purple gems. Hours passed that turned into days, which I'm sure had blurred into months. Throughout that entire time, Bell Maga managed to not stop talking. From everything she told me, the only thing that had stuck to my head was that she loved to travel and see new things. One day as we sat to make a fire and ate our green mini square meals, Bell Maga had mentioned how she was born in this huge laboratory in the City of Mars. She mentioned, "That is where all the special factions' members are born. The women that give birth to us died due to the high demand in nutrients we require during the whole birth process. The only thing that keeps women alive are the machines that the faction created to ensure women are receiving optimal amounts of nutrients until they die. Those women are honored and continue to be, for the end result is a *superior prodigy* like myself. My genetic makeup is perfect. When my time to be chosen comes, the faction will put the *supercells* inside of me and my other fellow prodigy sisters. One of us will give birth to an evolutionary life, far from being the likes of anything we have ever known." I did not like the way that sounded, and from the looks of it, Bell Maga completely bought into the idea. She had mentioned, "At birth they connected all the prodigies to nanomachines to ensure optimal nutrients were being fed to them." I almost felt as though she had been brainwashed by bullshit since Bell mentioned every thought since birth was about the ideologies of the emperor and their religious views on why the faction has been blessed by the God Llamas. At the time, I didn't care to hear anything more about the faction. They were all killers at the end of the day, now hiding behind their superior dogma bullshit.

The walking did not stop, but it definitely got colder. The tunnels were huge, and no telling really where we were heading. Bell Maga continued talking until I stopped and she bumped into me. I saw it in the distance three supermassive, giant levitating pillars. By the time we came closer to the pillars, they looked even bigger. I was awestruck and did not realize such a thing existed. When we got close enough, we heard a figure say, "Hello." The hooded figure looked at us and demanded to know what it was that we wanted. I began to feel like we were lost and wanted to return to the surface. The hooded figure smiled and replied, "Why would you want to go back up there when you belong here?" I looked at the figure, confused, until the hooded figure clapped both hands and a flame came into existence. I needed to learn how to do something like that. The dark hooded figure quickly was shown to be a woman with yellow braided hair and yellow eyes, and she said her name was *Sol.*

She mentioned, "We have seen what has been happening on the surface. We know what you carry inside your branded 23 number and what the prodigy standing next to you is destined to give birth to. Both of you, come this way to speak with her."

I was confused as usual and asked Sol, "What in the heck are you talking about?"

Sol mentioned, "Less talking, more walking."

I followed SOL thinking about what had just been mentioned. I began to look at Bell Maga a little differently. Was she something more important that I had failed to notice?

We made our way into the structure, passing under the levitating pillars; it was a little much for comfort. We walked up *the Great Wall of Steps* and, at the top of the stairs, found a flat platform that Sol said goes on for eternity in every direction we looked. According to Sol, we had stepped outside space and time and entered what the loud voice came to call *the Outside.* Everyone suddenly became visible; they were bowing to what they called the *Energy of Eve.* It was a floating white ball of pure energy.

Out of nowhere, Sol, from the side of me, said, "What you see before you is the original woman from the resistance of Eve who merged all their minds with what found Sheila. It was an *energy ball* that the faction created in their lab. It was accidentally stumbled upon by one of the faction's top minds, Dr. Smart."

I said, "No fuckin' way!"

Sol said, "I take it you know who I am talking about?"

I said, "Hell yes, I do! He saved my life, but sadly, he is now dead."

The woman said, "The great Dr. Smart discovered a way to play god. He tried creating a way to merge with the very thing that brought the cosmos into existence. It was noted that he attempted to fully merge with the energy ball, but it rejected him. It was never clear why, but the Last Government decided to put a rap to the experiment. Afterwards noted on file under 'Top Secret' in the faction system, the doctor noted in those few minutes of being merged to the energy ball he became one with all of existence. The faction deemed such a thing too dangerous and put it away. One day in one of our raids, a resistance fighter named Sheila came face-to-face with the energy ball. When she looked up, it was right before her, and then it shot into her brain, creating a white flash. She was the one that created all the tunnels and navigated all the women from the resistance down here. From there, she asked that we merge with her to become a part of something greater. Half of us joined the energy ball. The other half of the women decided to stand by its side. Over time the force of the energy ball grew even stronger from the will of the woman. It became even bigger and created the outside."

On that day, Sol mentioned, "It informed everyone to refer to it as the Energy of Eve. We knew this was the way, and from that day on, the rest of us were confident that we all had a higher purpose to serve in this life."

It was a lot of information to take in at once. Eve was talking. She said, "You need to hear what I have to say. The emperor at the end of the Space Wars held *President Von Vegas* captive. In order to receive all of the *Republics'* classified information, he forced Dr. Smart to merge the president's mind inside of him. The president's body was disposed of in one of the death trenches, and Emperor Hola was able to stay ahead of your parents' every move until they were captured. The thing you need to know is that President Von Vegas still lives inside of Emperor Hola. He has only been repressed. If you can find a way to help him permeate from the depths of Emperor Hola's mind, you might have a chance in defeating the emperor. The other thing you need to be aware of is that the woman standing next to you, Bell Maga, she can bring the end to this planet. She has the capacity to accept the supercells and give birth to the next evolutionary entity. This new entity will be like none other the world has seen. It still remains her choice on what she will decide now for you, 23, the matter of the Angel codes within you. I suggest you let them stay here in this place. Those codes are something that the emperor can't get his hands on. I can teleport you to the Angel, and you can destroy it before Emperor Fang's forces arrive. With the codes I can completely render the Angel useless. I do need to let you know that it is not going to be an easy task. Your friend 371 has been infected with a bacteria that has latched to his brain and driven him insane. Sadly, he is too far gone now to try and rescue. Know that you are going to be met with a lot of resistance. I allowed Eve to extract the codes from my 23 branding."

Eve had mentioned, "It was good that you didn't need to use a nanomosquito to extract the codes. It would have been very painful and left an itchy lump. It was pretty cool to see the coding of the Angel. It looked like a double helix embedded with coding. Eve absorbed the code and said she had shut down the Angel."

In that moment, Bell Maga came forward and said, "I did not want to be the prodigy that brought a new entity into this world that would bring destruction. I decided I wanted to have 23's genetic code placed inside of me instead. It was clear to me now that what the faction had been doing was wrong. The emperor is an evil man that needs to be stopped."

That was the first time I heard Bell Maga speak like that. It was the first time I noticed how beautiful her short silver hair was and how her robes were all silver as well. She had amazing silver eyes, and her mind was elite. She was already that special entity brought into existence. She had a demeanor to her that was young but also ahead of her time. I didn't realize until now how much I am actually attracted to her. Perhaps that's why I didn't want to listen to her. In the beginning, I was scared to get close to her. I was a young man, and she was a young prodigy woman. She already had the best of both worlds within her. She was the best of the faction population, and I was all that was left of mankind.

Eve spoke, "Is this what you choose, Bell Maga?"

She said, "Yes!" With the flash of a bright light, Bell was announced pregnant by Eve.

I was thrown back thinking that was not how I envisioned it, but that works. I knew what I had to do, and it started with making sure Bell stood safe here. The next thing I had to do was destroy the Angel then focus on bringing down the emperor. I looked at Eve and said I was ready. Eve informed me, when I was ready to return, to simply say her name. One final thing she mentioned.

I said, "What's that, Eve?"

She said, "This is for you."

Before I knew it, a pair of *golden laser daisho* was strapped to me. I said, "Thank you too Eve." She mentioned how my father, Mr. 22, was naturally gifted with his golden laser daisho. It brought a smile to my face.

XVII

Coward

I ARRIVED ON THE ANGEL. It was pitch-black from being shut down by Eve. Luckily, the oxygen was still functioning. The very first thing that I noticed was the view from the windows. There were so many stars. I took a peek out each window, each with its spectacular view. I walked to the other side of the hall, looked out, and saw a lot of space debris. It would appear that 371 had the Angel located around the remains of the former colonies. What massive space debris was left looming around. I again thought of my father at that moment. I continued to walk down the massive hall. It was difficult to navigate with how dark it was. I turned the corner and saw another massive hall. This Angel must be huge! I took my time searching throughout Angel for the command center. If I could detonate the Angel without bumping into 371, that would be just fine. I came across an area that must have been the green laboratory. I've never seen so many green trees, grass, vegetables. I continued my search and came across the cafeteria and noticed it had items on there that I have only ever dreamed of. There were hot pizza slices on the racks, hot dogs, sandwiches, actual chips, and soda. It was clear to me that 371 could have stayed up here for as long as he wanted. I made my way through the dormitory, and all the doors were locked. I continued and passed the restroom. It'd been a while since I had used toilet paper, so I felt the urge to use it. I washed my hands for a good while and did not want to touch my face and contract any kind of virus. At one point, I was honestly lost. I found my way down to the engineer room. I managed to get a front-eyes view of what makes this baby kick. I tried the control panels in this room, thinking I could find some sort of self-destruct button, but at the end, I really just poked at a bunch of buttons. I continued to walk and started to smell something funky. I made my way to the source, only to find fresh faction dead bodies. They must have beaten me by a good day or so.

Where was 371? I continued to make my way around. The littlest noises started to freak me out. I found the captain's chambers and walked inside. Everything had been tossed around as if someone was looking for something. I made my way out of the room and heard a loud bang. I could feel the vacuum of space pulling at me until I managed to grab something. I heard it again and again until I realized what was going on. The faction started to shoot at the Angel again. I had to find the control room and get the heck out of here. I made my way down the hall, and I heard a voice that was 371's. I looked through the mini glass window on top of the door and saw that it was him. He must have been no more than five feet tall and had a hunched back with two lumps. I saw that his robes were really just rags at this point and his feet were naked, exposing his crusty toes. His wild white hair that looked like the guy 444's would show me who they called Albert Einstein. I did not see that he was armed, so I decided to walk in and try to talk to him.

As I made my way in, he asked, "Who goes there?" I noticed he could no longer see. I did not answer him, and with another step, I made my way toward him. He threw a *burgundy laser kunai* at me. If it wasn't for my enhancement of speed, I would have taken that straight to the head.

I finally decided to speak and said, "It is me, 23!"

371 said, "Ah yes! The boy with the codes. Do you have the codes with you? For with them I can initiate the full power of Angel and blow up the wretched *star*. Nobody deserves to exist. It is time to end it all."

I told him, "I can't let you do that."

His tone changed and said, "I thought you would understand after seeing everything the faction has done. Don't you see out these windows." He pointed at the debris from the space colonies, which did lend his case some weight. "He even pushed a button that showed the planets where mankind had created other planetary colonies."

371 said, "Look at them. They are all gone living in the nuclear winter. Only monsters do these kinds of things."

I told him, "Monsters also blow up stars."

He looked at me and said, "We all know everything eventually comes to an end."

I took another step, and immediately he shot his kunai in front of my foot. His tone changed again when he said, "You were not there at the end of the Space Wars. I, along with others, abandoned our duty to protect the captain and his family. We swore allegiance to the *Golden Star* of the ten colonies. The Golden Star was an order of elite, specially hand-selected members. After seeing so many of our fellow order members being murdered by the faction, a lot of us made a run for it."

"You were cowards. Say what you want about my actions, but you were not there, boy. The Order of the Golden Star formed when Colony One was built. The order had protected every captain from Mr. 001 to Mr. 22. We fought off multiple enemy forces as the space colonies doubled in numbers from one to eventually ten. Our headquarters were located on colony one. It was a huge rectangle that went all the way up to the ceiling of the colony. At the very center of that rectangle was a huge golden emblem that showed the star of the order."

"Let me guess, the building you are describing was all white?"

371 gave a sinister smile. "Yes! We had a headquarters on the planet Rump for when MR. 22 needed to go speak with President Von Vegas."

I said out loud, "The building in the ruins…you knew the *black hole weapon* was there, didn't you?"

371 responded with a huge grin, "I did! I was enthralled by the idea of having you go there to set it off without you actually knowing what you were doing. I figured you were so naive and looking for answers that you would be easy to manipulate. I can say it was so amazing to see the detonation from space. It was a beautiful chaos,

such destructive force to have witnessed. To have even seen part of the supercontinent be erased was a spectacular bonus."

The Order of the Golden Star had been blinded to the imminent attack from the faction. The order saw themselves unconquerable. The day the faction attacked the headquarters, the order felt that was the day when the Space Wars began. A few faction soldiers had taken a ship on a one-way kamikaze attack. They exploded the ship upon impact, and the golden emblem fell from the sky as the building collapsed. All the residents of Colony One were distraught. No one had experienced war for some time due to many years of peace. Toward the final ending moments of the Space Wars, when shit really hit the fan and the shooting got nasty, that is when I made a run for my life. I betrayed my order and the oath that I swore. I knew there was no turning back for me. I hopped on a capsule and made my way to Angel knowing she could be my salvation. When I arrived with the few other AWOL order members, we saw that Mr. 22 had just gotten done branding someone with his golden laser daisho. The branding on the man's chest read "Five hundred." From what we saw, he had been teleporting men to the planet of Rump. Immediately I had figured he must have implanted the codes to Angel within his branding, and within moments, the few men with me chased after him. He must have known of our intentions since his sense of IQ in pernicious situations, including on the battlefield, had no equal. He acted on pure instinct. He grabbed a black remote, hit the gold button, and was teleported. I knew I had lost a golden opportunity, but I also knew I had the power of the Angel at my hands. I may not have had the codes to access the full potential of Angel, but I knew it would only be a matter of time before they surfaced. I, along with the few other members, immediately discovered why Mr. 22 was in such a hurry to get off Angel. Aside from us, multiple faction members had caught up, those who were tailing Mr. 22. They thought us with him, and all hell broke loose. At the end of that scrimmage, only I survived and decided to take a peek into the Angel supercomputer. I quickly jumped into the president's network to witness him in his office confronted by Emperor Fang and his soldiers. The president had been betrayed by some of his bodyguards. They had been promised so much more within the faction.

The emperor said, "At long last, the fall of the Republic, President Von Vegas's final words were 'Mankind shall prevail!'" Emperor Hola knocked him out with a shot straight to the center of his face. They took his body, and the system went black. I fell to my knees, witnessing the fall of the Republic and the rise of an evil emperor.

I knew my time would come one day. His tone of voice changed again. He threw a pure golden star at me and said, "Start the order again to protect Rump and its people!" At that moment, his voice changed yet again for the final time, and a whole different person was present in the room. He spoke, and immediately I knew who it was, he who gave me that evil smile. "Long time no see, 23." The emperor had taken over 371's mind. The emperor said, "I always knew I could not find Angel, but I figured my top scientist could. Dr. Smart came up with the brilliant idea of spreading nanobacteria throughout space where we thought Angel might be hiding. Dr. Smart engineered the nanobacteria to seek out a human host, and once it infected the host, it would connect with its brain, giving us full control over those infected. I was curious to hear out what 371 would tell you, and from the sounds of it, nothing worth of value. What I am pleased to know is, this will be where you fall, 23."

The very next moment, the emperor had me by the shoulders. He smiled. "Do you like the upgrade that we installed to this pathetic human?"

He threw me against the wall and said, "This golden laser daisho is quite impressive," after swiftly taking them from me; he punched a whole into one of the ship's windows and threw my daisho out in the vacuum of space. He came at me again and punched me in the stomach. He grabbed me by the hair and spun me around the room until he let go. He was smiling the whole time that bloodlusted look began to show itself.

The emperor grabbed me by the leg and slammed me to the ground. I felt that one; he began to laugh out loud. "Finally, the last man in existence. I am going to take pride in this." He came at me again, this time using a boxer's fighting style to deliver some heavy blows to my body. I was coughing up blood and felt myself getting worn down. I decided, with the energy I had left, I made a run for it down the hall. I could hear the emperor screaming at the top of his lungs, coming after me; he had gone mad. He chased me down as he rammed me through the wall that read "The Garbage Department." He smiled and said, "When I open these doors releasing everything into space, that will be your salvation."

I stood up with a dizziness that I had not felt in a while. I took a step back, falling on my butt. "What a display of weakness from your species. You were all destined to go extinct one day." He picked me up by my head and punched me in the throat. "To think you ever had a chance is laughable. This body I possess will be the sacrifice that will end the line of humanity." He threw me at one of the walls.

371's body walked over to the lever and asked me for any last words. I screamed, "YES! Mr. *President Von Vegas*, please help me immediately." The emperor grabbed his head. I screamed again with desperation in my voice, "Mr. President, please help me!" I could clearly see the struggle taking place. I got up with all the energy I had left. I grabbed a piece of pipe that was on the ground that had collapsed from the wall and went running at 371's body. Still scream-ing, "Mr. President, please help me!" I stood before 371 and started swinging at his head and kept swinging until there was nothing left to hit. The emperor had played dirty and lost. I could see the other ships from the faction arriving from the windows and made my way back to the command room. I jumped on the supercomputer and put on a thirty-second detonator. As the timer ticked away, the fac-tion boarded the Angel and right as they had reached me and started shooting at me with their laser guns. I yelled, "*Eve*," name-teleport-ing my way out of there, and saw the explosion of the Angel spread out into the vacuum of space.

XVIII

Revelation

I ARRIVED BACK AT THE Outside and saw Bell talking with a few of the other women, including Sol. She looked even more amazing since the last time I had seen her beautiful silver hair. I gripped my fist, holding the Order Golden Star, promising I would wear this with pride. I knew what I wanted to tell Eve. I told Eve, "I have no weapon to battle the emperor left. Can one of the women tip off one of the remaining Dark Faction members that I am down here, and when they arrive, we will ambush them right as they approach the Great Wall of Steps." Eve sent one of her most trusted women from the group of Sol to provide the intel to one of the remaining Dark Faction members. After two days of waiting, one finally arrived. They passed through the entrance path of the giant levitating pillars, and I knew it was game-face time.

I finally came face-to-face with another member of the Dark Faction. I remember 444 telling me about the Dark Faction member *Fear*. She was a woman about five foot ten in height, bold except for the little black ball of hair on the top of her bold head. She wore a black thong with spiked boots and wore only a sleeveless black leather jacket. From what I heard, she actually had the most kills under her belt from all the other Dark Faction members. She was the real deal, and there was no mistaking it. She was a woman of few words and was fearless. She had eyes that were completely red in honor of the emperor, and her signature weapon was the *black laser sansetsukon*, or as many like to call it, the three-section staff. She told me, "You must be really dumb to be just out in the open with no one around."

I told her, "I am a slow learner."

She smiled. "What fortune has befallen me. The final man left in existence, and I get to hand over his head to the emperor."

I smiled. "Don't you know that I am also the last member to the Order of the Golden Star," and showed her the *golden star* I had on my chest.

She laughed so hard it could be heard from some distance. "Give it a rest, kid. You are young and naive to the events that have unfolded."

I smiled back and noticed she was not thrilled that I was still smiling. "Like I said, I am a hard learner."

Fear said, "Enough of this nonsense. Time to say goodbye."

I put my hand up and told her to stop. I said, "You are wrong. I have grown, and now what I desire is your weapon. Please hand it over nicely."

Fear said, "You must have gone nuts with everything that has happened."

I told Fear, "I just know now more than ever what I am fighting for." I raised my other hand, and from above the Great Wall of Steps surrounded all around us were women with white laser bow and arrows pointing at Fear.

Out loud, she said, "No fuckin' way, and here I thought this was my catch of the century. Nonetheless, a warrior like myself can't be captured."

The next thing I knew, Fear ran at me as fast as she could, and again before I knew it, she was at my feet full of laser arrows with many holes in her body, blood spreading throughout the floor. She had taken all those arrows head-on and still had managed to touch my feet, truly fearless until the very end.

It wasn't enough for me to leave the last faction member alive. I was focused and determined to avenge mankind. As I bent over to grab the black laser sansetsukon from Fear's dead body, a red laser harpoon was shot at my chest. A second later, I was yanked all the way past the entrance of the three massive floating pillars now behind me.

Guilt spoke to me, saying, "Did you really think we did not suspect a trap? I even took the liberty to create a red force field around us. No one is going to be able to help you now, 23." He took the red laser harpoon out of my body, and I felt the heavy pain. Guilt was obesely fat. His stomach hung out of his sleeveless green shirt with a mini pocket. He had black teeth that were also crooked and wore a pair of blue cut-up jogging shorts. I had never seen someone with such a big fat foot walking around in bowling shoes. He had a tattoo of a red pineapple on his stomach and wore a black collar around his neck that spelt out *guilt*.

I asked him, "Is that the best you got?"

Guilt started to speak to me, as I could see outside the field all the women running to try to come to my aid, including Sol, but halted due to the red force field.

He told me, "You should consider yourself lucky to have come this far. The last of mankind will go down in the history books by saying Guilt from the Dark Faction killed the last man on Rump whom they called 23."

"There was a doctor in his younger days who had created all the laser weapons we know of today that exist. In those days, he was proud to produce new inventions for the faction. These laser weapons, do you even know why they have different colors, 23? It is because Dr. Smart found out how to harness the energy being given off by different-colored stars in the universe. Dr. Smart, in those days, was given unlimited access to anywhere he desired, accompanied by the Last Government to do whatever he wanted. They built him a lab in each of the four major faction cities in case he needed immediate access based on a project he may have been working on. He was untouchable. His inventions were so evolutionary that the emperor kept pushing him until he started using him for pure evil, like the experiments on mankind that eventually ate him up inside. You want to know who was the one responsible for the capture of your father, 23? Once he beamed down to Rump from the Angel, it was Dr. Smart with the intel he had been given, captured a man branded 77 on the back of his neck. The good doctor brainwashed him using dark nanoparticles. 77 became the ultimate sleeper mole. One day they placed him in the northern City of V, where intel the Last Government gathered had mentioned Mr. 22 was operating out of. With the dark nanoparticles, they were able to see and hear on screens, every one of 77 moves. 77 did indeed find Mr. 22 on the outskirts of the city. That man befriended your father, Mr. 22, took him back to his headquarters, which had been in a giant gold mine, about a good eighty strong men had been serving under your father. After some time passed, your father started sending 77 out with the other men on guerrilla attacks against the faction. In those moments is when we would activate 77 using the Salsa Verde Satellite and have him slaughter all the men he was with and then have him walk back to the gold mine as the lone survivor. One day, enough intel had been collected, and it was decided by the Last Government and the emperor they would attack the mine in the middle of the night. What they did first was activate 77 when everyone was asleep. He took out the guards covering the night duty watch then gave us the exact coordinates to the mine. It was too easy. By the time Mr. 22 was made aware of what was going on by all the laser gun fire, 77 tells your father to follow him to safety, leading him straight into the hands of the Last Government."

It was tough to hear how Dr. Smart was responsible for so much, yet in the end, he tried to make up for it. I actually wish I could even ask for his help right now. Then Guilt laid one more thing on me, "You know why you have brain damage, 23? It's because of one of the guerilla missions you went on with 77 and the other four men. It was in the middle of the night all six of you men were around the area of the City of Earth. Your mission that night was to set off an explosive that would kill thousands of faction members. You guys had taken a quick break three hours before the attack. 77 had mentioned he was going to scout the area to make sure no guards were in the area. When he was a good distance away, we activated him. We had already left him in the bushes a red laser sniper rifle. He set it up, and the first person he shot through the head was the man who was on watch with the number 1 on his left cheek. The other man happened to be nearby napping when he stood up without his shirt. He took the red laser straight through his heart, where he had 366 branded. You stood up and started wondering what was going on as you walked around you came to see your dead fellow comrades. 77 had you in his sights. He fired, and 9 jumps in front of you. From the angle the shot was taken, it looked like the laser had gone through the both of your heads. As you stumbled off from being pushed by 9, you fell from the cliff that was nearby. 77 was ordered to not check on you since you were presumed dead from the fall. We all have a story, 23, and yours just happens to deal with a lot of loss. It's okay, though, because I am going to free you from this world."

Guilt's fat self walked up to me and stepped on my hand. I yelled in pain, then he grabbed me by the hand and bit off my middle finger. I started screaming, and he began laughing as he swallowed my finger, my blood all around his face. He said, "I told you, 23, how did you think this was going to end for you?" He sat on me as I lay there helpless, feeling my body being crushed by something that felt like a thousand pounds. I felt a few ribs crack. All the woman could do was watch due to the force field. I could see Sol full of tears. Guilt put my motionless body on a wagon he had brought with him. He said, "This is where you will be freed, 23. Once I light this wagon on fire, I couldn't lift my body and had no way of defending myself." What I did hear was a voice in my head telling me to say the words. Guilt said, "It is time for you to say goodbye." He walked up to me, kissed me on the head, and said, "Farewell, 23."

I said indeed and yelled, "GOLDEN STAR LASER!" My Golden Star shot a golden laser through Guilt's face, and he dropped dead.

I quickly found myself surrounded by a ton of women assisting me off the wagon. I asked for a drink of beer, and I was informed by Sol I did not want to start that habit. I let Sol know how tiresome this had all become. They took me back to *the Beyond* to be patched up by Eve. After some time, I started to feel my strength coming back to me. I saw Eve approach me, and she told me I had gotten careless. I said that how I have approached things since day one.

I asked Eve, "What would be the next best course of action now?"

She told me, "To finish what I have started."

I told Eve, "I don't think I have what it takes to defeat the emperor."

Eve followed up with, "*Fear is the most powerful enemy of reason.*"

I told Eve, "What more can I do?"

Eve told me, "Plenty."

I did not know how to respond to that answer, but nonetheless, I had to figure something out. I spent a few days trying to figure out a way to bring down Emperor Fang, but nothing came to mind. I tried meditating on it, walked around in circles. I even went days without having taken a shower, until Bell forced me to. I even ate some apples from the apple tree. The Beyond was an infinite place where just about any manifestation you thought of came to reality, which was a pretty cool feature to have at my disposal.

I found myself lying out on a flattened surface until some turtles started walking over me. I kept thinking and thinking and thinking for who knows how long, since the Beyond is a place Eve created outside space and time. I was lying in one of my manifestations where I created a pool of red wine. I was able to enjoy myself and pour myself up a glass anytime. I would be in a thinking pod, still working out those thoughts. I had gotten in so deep that Bell came to check on me. She had told me she never saw me go this far into the Beyond. She feared I would venture too far and not know how to return. I told Bell I just needed some time to think and create a solid plan to defeat the emperor. She kissed me on the cheek and walked away.

Some more time had passed, and still nothing. I had a thick black mustache growing, and my black hair had grown into what looked like a giant bush on my head. My skin was tanned, and I had a caramel glow going. I had decided while thinking I would practice using the black laser sansetsukon. I allowed myself to think of my surrounding area as a place where I was being attacked by faction members. All at once, I had hundreds coming at me and with my newly acquired weapon. I spent hours slaying them all until I fell to the ground light-headed. I decided to change the scenery, finding myself getting a back massage.

More time had passed, and I felt like I had gotten taller, browner, stronger, wiser until I found myself back in the darkness. I had forced the Beyond to manifest from my mind the darkness that I feared. I was surrounded in utter darkness, but I was no longer afraid. I had made up my mind that my focus would be unmatched, for I was hungry now more than ever. I grabbed the Golden Star I had with me from the order and threw it in front of me as far as I could. The star got bigger and bigger and bigger until I was covered in light. I could hear a voice calling me to come forward. I approached the direction the voice was coming from until I saw the voice take a human form that looked like a woman. It glowed with all golden robes. I could see the woman had eyes of gold, and the light surrounding her was very pure. The woman said, "You can either choose to bring an end to the emperor, or you can choose to live your life out."

I said, "I want to bring an end to the emperor."

The voice said, "Step forward," so I took my step forward.

A blinding light hit me when I was able to see again. The woman began fading away, and she told me, "Wear it proudly."

I looked at myself, and I found myself wearing all gold robes. I asked, as the last flickers of light began to fade away, who had granted me such a privilege.

The last dots of light said, "We did."

I asked, "Who are 'we'?"

The last dot of light said, "The former members of the Golden Star."

I made my way back to Eve and the others. When I had arrived, they had barely recognized me. I told them they made it seem like I had been gone forever. Bell wound up coming up to me and said, "You were gone for nine months."

I could tell, now looking at Bell, that she looked like she was ready to deliver. I had asked if a name had been given yet. Bell said no, that she was waiting for me. I asked for the gender of the baby. Bell mentioned it was going to be a girl. I had one name come to mind right away: 24. Bell spent some time cutting my hair until it was short again. She put something in my hair, and I had a mini-spiky-hair look going. She looked into my eyes and mentioned she never realized how brown my eyes were. I could tell she had finally decided to ask me what I was going to do. I mentioned I was going to take a large space shift and ram it into the emperor's golden palace and end his reign. Bell asked me one final question. She asked, "Would it cost you your life?"

I told Bell Maga, "I'm not sure."

She told me, "Then make sure to give it all you got!"

XIX

Havoc

I SPOKE TO EVE TO have her teleport me to the nearest spacecraft. I had informed her of my plan, and she had ordered a handful of women to go with me. She let me know, if anything was to happen to me, she would take care of Bell and the newborn 24. I waved goodbye to Bell and told Sol she better watch over her for me. Before I knew it, we were back in the City of Taste, still dismantled from the previous incident with the Angel. We were teleported by one of the hangers and came across a pretty big cargo ship that was named *The Ozark II*. We all jumped on. I put the cargo ship on cruise control and ran through the plan with the team one more time. I would say I had a team of ten women ready to lay their lives on the line. I let them know when we crashed through the front of the palace to right away form the first line of defense with five women. We made ourselves up to the second-floor hall to set up the second line of defense with three women laying down fire and had the last two women come with me. Everyone was stacked on board. Everyone had a laser assault rifle, grenades, and Eve had given them each a *gold laser sai*. We also had the cargo ship set to a thirty-minute timer to detonate in case we failed to kill the emperor.

As we approached the golden palace, we could see a giant statue of an enforcer named Delta at the front of the palace doors. There was a silence among us for several minutes. The wind was all that could be heard, and then the woman started strapping up their golden robes. We decided we would go in as the *New Order of the Golden Star*; across our golden robes centered to our chest laid an even brighter Golden Star. On the golden laser shields we carried on our backs, we also had the Golden Star imprinted. I took it to the next level and used some of the war paint to draw a golden star on my forehead. Everyone else decided to wear golden bandannas; we were focused and knew what needed to be done. I closed my eyes for a second and left all other affairs outside my mind. I knew we would only get one chance at this.

We were about forty-five seconds from impact. We braced ourselves. Someone had brought with them what apparently used to be referred to as an iPod and a beats pill. They played a song called "Back on Something" by *Clyde Carson*. The woman whom we called *Deluxe* said rap and hip-hop were two of her favorite genres from the American times. She immediately reminded me of 444 and his taste for the Americans. I also barely remembered I needed to go feed *Alaska*. She must be starving.

While in the air fifteen seconds from impact, we could tell we had caught the palace off guard. By the time they had gotten to their .50-cal. laser to shoot us down, it was too late. Ten seconds from impact, I can feel the energy in the cargo ship. Five seconds, we knew we had caught them snoozing and would have enough time to set up our barriers. One second, then a massive collision was felt. Before I knew it, all happened so fast; we were already on the second floor, and Deluxe and the other woman we called *Cerveza* were both at my side walking down the hall with me. We could hear the laser fire commencing from behind us as we moved forward with precision and vindication. We came across some fire, and Deluxe got in a few headshots for us. This second floor was huge and had many different areas to it as we continued to make our way. Cerveza had some headshots under her belt as well. Things were happening quickly. As we walked, making our way to the emperor's throne, half of the floor collapsed as a trap, and Cerveza fell to the ground full of spikes meeting her end. We kept moving with our eyes wide open until we finally arrived at Emperor Hola. He was sitting on his golden throne chair the size of the whole wall. I looked around, surprised there were no guards with him.

Emperor Hola mentioned, "For some time now I have been waiting for you. How proud I am of you to allow me this moment." I looked at him a bit with a hard stare. He said, "I killed your father, Mr. 22. I had your mother turned into an abomination, and now I have the chance to end the line of man."

The emperor stood up from his golden throne and said, "I wish that you had brought more bodies with you." He jumped in the air so fast that when he came down, he crushed Deluxe through the second floor, instantly killing her from the sheer force of the impact. I jumped down and saw a familiar look on the emperor's face. That bloodlusted look in his eyes had turned red again, and his body was super buffed out. He had torn off his golden robes; this time he had his whole white body, from bald head to toe, covered in tattoos, on his entire chest, leading down to his abdomen. He had an image of a kingdom on fire with dead bodies by his abdomen that represented mankind. On his back, he had the image of space and, within it, images of the ten colonies shattered to pieces, including images of nine dead planets that had been nuked. The emperor made it crystal clear that he was the bringer of death and destruction. He stood up and grabbed the laser shield from Deluxe's destroyed body, including her golden laser sai, and the emperor ran at me. I took out my now golden laser sansetsukon, and immediately sparks from the impact could be seen going everywhere. He looked at me, surprised to see the three-section staff in my possession. He smiled, saying I was in for a treat as he came running at me again.

This time upon the sheer force of the impact, it threw us in separate directions, going through the walls. The impact can be heard from across the floor that another woman we called *Sprite* from the order came to assist me. I asked her how things were looking, and she said the other order members had things under control. She had charged in the direction that the emperor had been thrown and had managed to lay a blow to Emperor Fang's left pectoral muscle with her golden sai. I looked at my golden laser sansetsukon, which had been destroyed from the impact. I took out my golden laser shield and ran at Emperor Hola full speed, taking him straight through another wall. Sprite, right away with both of her sai, thrust them through the emperor's stomach. This really pissed him off, and he grabbed both of Sprite's hands and crushed them. When he stood up, he took both of her sais and thrust them through her chest, killing her immediately.

He looked at me, smiling, telling me, "You are next."

Little did Emperor Hola know that when he was lying on the ground, having been stabbed by Sprite, I threw a grenade his way. Right as it went off, I dived to the ground. A massive explosion took place. I stood up and saw that Emperor Hola was missing his whole right hand. It was actually pretty funny to me and brought a smile, including seeing him covered in blood. The emperor began yelling as he ran at me punching me, sending me flying back into the palace's main hall, where we had crashed the cargo ship. The emperor walked my way with such a monstrous demeanor you could tell from his facial expression he indeed enjoyed the battle. The thing he had failed to realize was that the firing had stopped, and the two other women stood in front of him from the order. They had managed to kill all of Emperor Fang's guards, and now they were the last two women standing from the firefight, *Lexus* and *Diamond*. Emperor Hola smiled. "It doesn't matter if you have defeated my forces here at the palace, because other reinforcements are already on their way."

The three of us started laughing. Lexus let him know this was pretty much a one-way mission, in that the cargo ship has enough firepower to level a quarter of this city. Diamond mentioned at this point I'd imagine there about a good five minutes left. The emperor smiled at the idea, saying, "Death is inevitable."

Emperor Fang followed with, "You may think you have won, but in the City of V lies my successor, my contingency plan in case I ever fell. He would be activated from his cryochamber the moment I was to die. The faction will continue to rule, and there is not a damn thing you can do about it, for you three will die here with me."

That is when Diamond had heard enough and ran at the emperor with her sai. She managed to stick him in the kidney area. He grabbed her hand and pulled out her sai then shoved her aside with a massive shoulder to her stomach, knocking the wind out of her. Emperor Fang came my way, and Lexus, halfway through, tackled him through the wall leading into what looked like a dining room area; that was when Emperor Fang grabbed her and, with such force, threw her through the table. He turned around, and I tackled him into what appeared to be the kitchen of the palace. We went at it again, hand-to-hand combat, each delivering blows to the other body and face. He kicked me with such force to the chest that it sent me flying outside into the patio with a swimming pool. He came behind me and started choking me out. Diamond thrust the SAI straight through his back, letting go of his grip on me. He stood up and took the sai out of his back. Had he been anybody else, they would have been paralyzed. The emperor mentioned how he made enhancements to himself as well. He smiled and yelled out, "Full power!" His muscles grew to an even bigger size. Diamond and I looked at each other and made a run for it back to the cargo ship to grab a laser gun. The emperor, even in this form, moved pretty fast and had been right behind us when we reached the cargo ship. Lexus flew at Emperor Hola with a glass blade that had broken off from the ship, landing right where his heart should be.

It did its damage, but the emperor kept smiling, saying, "You just don't get it, do you?" He took it out and threw it like a spear straight at Lexus, hitting her straight in the leg. "I am not human. You think and operate within human aspects. I am the emperor of the faction. We have evolved beyond you primitive beings."

Emperor Hola again came toward me, and Diamond jumped in front of him, landing several blows to his body, bringing him down to one knee. She used her speed and combative knowledge to lay a barrage of blows to Emperor Hola until he stood up again in a rage, kicking her with such force through the cargo ship. I ran at Emperor Hola, busting out some of the golden laser shuriken I had on me, throwing them all straight to his face, landing one in his eye, having him scream out. I took that time to charge him head onto the master stairs in the hallway leading up to the second floor. It was there where I began to punch the life out of him with every blow I landed to his face. I heard Lexus yell at me, saying, "Catch!" She tossed me the glass blade, putting it straight through his bald tattooed forehead. I stumbled back and fell down the stairs, exhausted from all the action. It would appear all three of us were worn-out with no energy left to move. I thought of Bell and began to wonder what she was doing. I began to cry out to her, saying, "I wish I was there to spend time with you." We could hear the reinforcements entering the palace. The next thing I knew, I heard a noise with the flash of a white light that led to a massive explosion clearing things out for a good quarter of the city.

XX

Deceit

I OPENED MY EYES AND saw I was back at the Outside. I was on a medical bed in bandages. I looked around and saw Diamond and Lexus lying beside me, recovering as well. I saw that Bell was at my bedside as well with a smile on her face, seeing that I was up. I told her that I did not understand what had happened. That was pretty much a one-way mission. I heard a familiar voice speak. Eve said, "It was I who could not let the three of you die in that explosion. I saw how committed you were to your cause. I also made that decision final after I heard Emperor Fang mention he had a successor ready as his contingency plan. I used the last of my energy to bring you guys here."

I said, "Why would you do that? Your power is needed way more than what us three could do!"

Eve said, "Not entirely true. Together you guys were strong. I suggest to you rebuild the order temple, have the Golden Star raised again, and have the order fight for the people. There are even faction individuals, believe it or not, that don't believe in what the Last Government was doing that would come to your side. One enemy has fallen, and sometime in the near future, the rise of this new successor will become apparent. You will need all the help that you can get." Eve began to disappear. "Protect this place. It belongs to all of you now. The Order of the Star will rise again."

Bell began crying, "Farewell, Eve. Thank you for everything. You have given us so much to fight, for I promise I will not let you down either."

"I did not know how much time we had before this new successor began to make his presence known, but I know we have to be ready for anything, and right now with the death of the emperor and the fall of the Last Government, everything has been thrown into chaos. Multiple parties were now fighting for power over the government. In the meantime, it allowed me to work with Lexus and Diamond on rebuilding the new temple. They were informing me about the intel they had gathered that was going on within the major cities."

When someone started yelling out that the baby was coming, by the time I ran over and got to the nursery, Bell was holding 24. She had such a beautiful smile with black hair and gray eyes, weighing about nine pounds. It had brought me such joy to see my daughter smiling at me. I went from being alone to now having a family and friends. I need to ensure we have a way of protecting everything I love.

At that moment, a nanobutterfly was flying around me, and it said, "Grab me."

I looked a bit surprised, but did as I was told. Then a very familiar voice began to speak; it was Dr. Smart! He said his humanoid faction mind (if we want to call it that) is so spread out in the net of data of these times that he can distribute a piece of himself wherever he wants. Dr. Smart went on to say he wanted to see me in private.

I looked at Bell. She nodded, and I said, "Okay."

Doctor Smart said, "Now eat the butterfly."

I grabbed it and put it in my mouth and ate it. Next thing I know, I was up in the mountains somewhere in front of an enormous white mansion hanging beautifully off the side of the mountain, going into the heart of the mountain. I heard a voice inside me belonging to Dr. Smart, saying, "Walk forward through the brown door after punching in the code 90210." I walked through after putting in the code and was amazed how much bigger the mansion was from the inside. I saw he had way more androids this time working various parts of the mansion. One of the androids came up to me and asked if I wanted a cup of tea. I said, "I am good for now," over the telecom installed in the mansion.

I could hear Dr. Smart saying, "Come up to my lab."

I saw a spiral staircase going up the side of a mountain. In the middle of the mansion, it looked pretty amazing. When I finally got to the top, I was greeted with a hot towel by an old friend, Bingo, who decided he wanted a hug, since it had been a while since we last saw each other.

I asked Dr. Smart, "Why didn't you just install something more convenient than ten flights of stairs?"

He looked at me differently from before, saying, "It was a good workout, right?"

Doctor Smart immediately began chatting it up, saying, "I transferred my data, a.k.a. as my humanoid brain, into another one of my humanoid clones that I have spread throughout Uno." Dr. Smart then led with, "The next time I set off a *black hole bomb*, give me some heads-up there. It is not cool to be sitting on your favorite chair with your favorite pepperoni pizza, finding yourself getting sucked into a black hole. There were some valuable items I lost, like my favorite chessboard."

I quickly apologized, "I really thought you were dead, but I should have known someone with your intellect would have contingencies."

Dr. Smart looked at me some type of way, saying, "I am not thrilled to be presenting myself in this humanoid form. My all-purple hair is touching the floor. I don't like that my hands are so massive and yet I have small feet. What's worse is that my butt is completely flat. My height is not cool. I don't like being shorter than six feet, but this will do for now. I am not digging that I have crooked teeth, let alone I am as skinny as a stickman. I don't mind this X-Men T-shirt and regal blue jeans with this cool *just-as-rich hat* I found lying around, but I also don't like that I have freckles all over my black chest."

Dr. Smart got down to business. "I know by now that you are aware of all the bad things I have done and all the good things I am now trying to do."

I said, "Yes!"

"Perfect," said Dr. Smart.

I am aware of this successor that the Emperor Fang was talking about. I asked, "How did you know that?"

Dr. Smart said, "I have eyes and ears everywhere." He said, "I had a couple of nanospiders at the emperor's golden palace watching the whole thing go down."

I asked him, "Why did it take you so long to reappear? I could have used your help multiple times."

"I am going to get to that. There is a power source located somewhere in the City of V. That source is what is powering this planet's core. If this new successor were to find its location, he could use it to destroy the planet or control the planet. Also, he is going to be in hiding for some time. Now that I am sure he is out of the cryochamber, he is going to need time to feed in order to gain his strength."

"What do you mean *feed*?"

Dr. Smart mentioned that on his hands, there appeared these highly advanced nanosuckers that drained the bodies of the vitamins of all their genetic code. "His name is still currently unknown to me, but rumors are out there that other humanoid faction members have slowly begun to come up missing."

I said, "How can I stop such a thing?"

Dr. Smart said, "Are you not the guy that is rebuilding the Order of the Star?"

"*Yes, I am!* But currently there are only three of us."

Dr. Smart smiled, saying, "You are still only thinking like a human I see, PANDA!" An android appeared from the lab. Dr. Smart said, "Here is your fourth member. He is my newest android. The best that I have built up to today."

I reached out my hand and said, "Nice to meet you." Panda shook mine with a strong grip. I asked Panda, "Are you up to swearing your *allegiance* to the Order of the Golden Star?"

Panda looked at me and said, "Sure, why not? It gets me out of this place."

I looked at Dr. Smart and said, "You really built a fine one here."

Dr. Smart stopped smiling and got serious for a second. "I want you to know there are other humanoids like myself that are willing to help you. A lot of them were too scared to help while the emperor was alive, but now that they know he is dead, you have allies, 23, know that. Be careful with 24. The emperor knew that Bell was with you and somehow found out that you had gotten her pregnant. You have a mole in your circle and will have to tread lightly, until you discover who it is. Also be careful because that should have really angered the emperor but he let it be for a reason. It's not normal that Bell desires changed. Don't you think it was a bit odd that she went from being a big believer in her cause to accept the supercells to then wanting to defy the emperor?"

I asked, "How did you know that?"

Dr. Smart smiled. "Still a slow learner, I see. I had nano-ants following you while you guys were in the tunnels talking."

I did start to think about what he was telling me. Dr. Smart was making a valid point.

Dr. Smart said, "Anyways, for now, take Panda with you. I will show you where I can help you put the new temple for the order as well. I know you have been putting in some work on building the temple with Lexus and Diamond, but scratch that your technology is outdated, and I will bring my subject matter expert with me."

I asked, "Who is that?"

He said, "The architect who designed and built this phenomenal mansion. My other android, *Hawk*."

I laughed out loud. "Go figure." I asked Dr. Smart one more thing.

He said, "What?"

I asked him if he had that purple pen.

Dr. Smart had to think about it for a good minute, then recalled that he walked over to one of his chairs where his all-white lab coat was and grabbed the purple pen out his pocket. He approached me and said, "Be smart on how I use this purple pen. Its power is limitless, but understand the responsibility of holding this kind of energy."

I said, "Thank you, Dr. Smart. You know I have changed and know how to make smarter choices these days."

Dr. Smart smiled and simply waved as 23 walked away.

When 23 had finally left the premises, Dr. Smart began with a light laughter that grew into a heavy dark laughter. He was aware how naive 23 can be. On one of the lab tables was a device that read on it "Salsa Verde Control System." Doctor Smart walked over to the device and pushed the big green button that read "Power On." The machine powered on with a thunderous noise. Multiple screens turned on in front of Dr. Smart. The entire planet of Rump and its residents were in his sights. The doctor was looking for his creations, in particular the *humans of the future*. It was time to activate them to fulfill their purpose. Dr. Smart found them on the screen and had the *Salsa Verde Mega Satellite* lock onto their location. Dr. Smart then hit the black button that read "Coded Signal." On the screen before his eyes, he screamed in happy madness. He had his pawns on the board now, ready to fulfill his desires. A darkness loomed over the laboratory. Dr. Smart sent some of them to take care of the emperor's successor in the City of V. The doctor began to take his true form with a monstrous shadow and took an image on the walls of the laboratory. From the shadows, he began yelling, "*Bear*, I will find you and your little bear crew, and when I do, my pawns will finally end you."

Bingo walked into the laboratory bringing what was left of Emperor Hola's body. Dr. Smart was pleased, telling Bingo, "Excellent work." He had his nanomosquitoes drain all the remaining nanodata and had the information conformed into a red nanodata pill. When Dr. Smart swallowed the red pill, the nanodata immediately gave him the codes to all of the Last Government's *top secret* information and projects. There was something in particular he was looking for, and then he stumbled upon it, with such an evil smile.

About the Author

JOEL RIOJAS IS AN ARMY veteran who lives in Las Vegas, Nevada. Joel Riojas comes from a Hispanic background and has attained a bachelor's degree in social work from Bradley University. He has always expressed his creativity in many forms, drawing motivation from his son and family. His works include, but are not limited to, his clothing business "Just As Rich" and working with his cousin Antonio Santiago selling "toni olo coffee co." Joel has always visualized stories and finally found the opportunity to bring one of many to life.